Dreamer

Inspired by a true story

Dreamer

Inspired by a true story

By Cathy Hapka

Based on the motion
picture written by
John Gatins

Scholastic Inc.
New York Toronto London Auckland Sydney
Mexico City New Delhi Hong Kong Buenos Aires

No part of this publication may be reproduced in whole or in part, stored in a retrieval system, or transmitted in any form or by any means, electronic, mechanical, photocopying, recording, or otherwise, without written permission of the publisher. For information regarding permission, write to Scholastic Inc., Attention: Permissions Department, 557 Broadway, New York, NY 10012.

ISBN: 0-439-77494-2

TM & © 2005 Dream Works LLC

Published by Scholastic Inc.

SCHOLASTIC and associated logos are trademarks and/or registered trademarks of Scholastic Inc.

12 11 10 9 8 7 6 5 4 3   5 6 7 8 9 10/0

Designed by Pamela Darcy
Printed in the U.S.A.
First printing, November 2005

Dreamer

Inspired by a true story

Chapter 1

It was dawn in Kentucky. The rising sun painted a thin golden line along the horizon, casting its rays over miles of white fences and acres of lush bluegrass. Behind those fences sleek horses — broodmares, yearlings, stallions, and others — had spent the night grazing peacefully under the stars or dozing in roomy stalls. The area around Versailles, Kentucky, was steeped in the tradition of the Thoroughbred — filled with sprawling, immaculate farms where many Kentucky Derby winners or Breeders' Cup contenders had spent their early days frolicking in rolling pastures.

The sun's rays also illuminated a modest property with a weatherbeaten wooden sign reading CRANE HORSE FARM. In that neighborhood of immense acreages and multimillion-dollar stables, its dilapidated barn and small, weed-filled paddock seemed especially humble. The only thing fresh and new on the place was a sign that read FARM ACREAGE FOR SALE. But its poor condition wasn't the only difference between the Crane Horse Farm and its neighbors. It was also the only horse farm in the area with no horses in its barn or paddock.

In the smaller of the two homes on the property, eleven-year-old Cale Crane brushed her wavy blond hair out of her face and tiptoed down the creaky stairs. It was early — 4:40 A.M. according to the clock in her bedroom — and Cale could hardly keep her eyes open. She knew how her parents, Ben and Lilly, usually solved that problem — coffee. Today was going to be a big day for her, and she wanted to be awake for it.

The coffee didn't come out looking exactly like it did when her mother made it. It seemed strangely thick and gooey. Still, Cale figured it was pretty good for a first try. She poured herself a cup, sat down at the table, and glanced at the wall clock: 4:47.

Good. Her father would be up soon. Stifling a yawn, Cale waited. The familiar kitchen blurred and swam as her eyes drooped. She fought to stay awake.

When Ben Crane entered the kitchen a few minutes later, he saw his daughter sitting at the table, fast asleep, clutching a coffee cup in one hand. His weather-beaten face softened as he gazed at her for a moment.

Then he stepped around her, moving quietly as he poured himself a cup of the sludge from the coffeepot.

"Ben . . ." Lilly Crane's soft voice greeted him as she entered, still wearing her flannel nightgown. An older version of Cale with the same heart-shaped face and shoulder-length blond hair, Lilly was still beautiful despite the worry lines that creased her forehead those days.

Ben made a face and dumped the contents of his coffee cup into the sink. Then he glanced at his wife. "It might rain," he commented, keeping his voice low to avoid waking Cale.

"Pat said it would be a good day for me to come down to the diner," Lilly said quietly. "It'd just be breakfast and lunch three days a week."

Ben winced. It was a familiar topic, but not a welcome one. He nodded toward Cale, giving his wife a meaningful look.

Lilly understood. Stepping over to the table, she gently rubbed Cale's back. "Cale, why don't you head back upstairs?" she whispered.

Cale lifted her head and blinked up at her mother. Then she glanced toward her father. Still only half awake, Cale rose and shuffled out of the room.

When she was gone, Ben picked up where they had left off. "You know I'm not crazy about you gettin' a job at the diner. . . ."

Lilly didn't let him finish. "Well, Ben, *I'm* not crazy about the bank bills pilin' up — and there's another notice about the property tax." She grabbed the stack of bills and held them up for him to see.

"If you're working at the diner, who's with Cale all day?" he asked.

"Pop lives right next door," Lilly reminded him. "You two might not talk much, but Cale and he get along real well, and . . ." She paused, waiting for Ben to meet her eye.

He looked up. "And?" he asked.

"Ben, you've been tellin' her for months that you'd take her to work with you. Why do you think she's asleep at the table?"

Ben shook his head. "I know, Lilly," he replied, grabbing his keys. "And I will take her. But not today. I got a big race."

Lilly sighed. "What am I supposed to tell her?"

"Tell her I was running late and I couldn't wait for her to get ready." Ben was already moving toward the door. "I gotta go."

Lilly gazed after him as he left. She swallowed a sigh. Like so many other things about their life lately, this morning's little exchange had become painfully familiar.

Outside, Ben climbed into his ancient Ford pickup. He turned the key, and the engine sputtered into life with a few coughs and bangs. He was halfway down the driveway when something jumped in front of the truck.

Startled, Ben slammed on the brakes. It was only then that he recognized his daughter standing there staring at him defiantly. She was still in her pajamas, but she was holding jeans, a T-shirt, a pair of boots, and a baseball cap.

Hearing the squeal of brakes, Lilly stepped onto the porch to see what had happened. She hid a smile as Cale breathed hard, glaring at Ben as if daring him to drive around her. *She must have sprinted all the way out there from the house,* Lilly guessed.

In the truck, Ben sighed and shook his head. With a glance at his wife, he leaned out the window to speak to Cale.

"C'mon," he told her gruffly. "Get in. We're late."

Cale could hardly believe her ears. Despite her planning and determination, she had expected her father to find an excuse to leave her behind yet again. Doing her best to juggle the clothes, hat, and boots, she scurried alongside the truck. It wasn't until she was safely inside, leaning back against the tattered vinyl seat, that she dared to believe it.

She was going to the racetrack with her father!

Chapter 2

Cale got dressed in the truck as Ben drove along the two-lane highways of Versailles. She watched out the window as they passed one beautiful horse farm after another. There was Wishman Stables, the luxurious property currently owned by a Middle Eastern prince, with some of racing's current top names decorating the brass nameplates in its well-appointed barn. And there she could see the gates of Lane's End Farm, home of world-famous racehorse and stallion AP Indy and his stakes-winning son, Mineshaft, along with Belmont Stakes winner Lemon Drop Kid, top sire Kingmambo, and more than a dozen others. Nearby she knew was the turnoff for the road leading to Ashford Stud, which stood the great stallions Thunder Gulch, Fusaichi Pegasus, Giant's Causeway, Louis Quatorze, and many more. . . . Cale's grandfather had told her so many tales of the great horses who lived on these farms that she felt as if she knew all of them.

But she could tell that her father barely noticed the familiar scenery. He studied the horizon as he drove and shook his head.

"I don't like rain on race day," he muttered, more to himself than to Cale.

"It's not raining," Cale replied, choosing to look on the bright side. "The sun's coming out."

Ben glanced at her. "Okay," he said. "I hope you're right."

A few minutes later they arrived at Kentucky Fairgrounds Racetrack. The picturesque sweep of the grandstand filled Cale's eyes as she climbed out of the truck. It was early, and the stands were deserted. But she could almost hear the roar of the crowd and the excited shouts of the track announcer. . . . She sighed happily, still hardly believing she was there.

Ben led her through the parking lot and on to the backside, the area of the racetrack that was closed to the public. This was where the horses lived while at the track to train or race; it was a private world of horses and owners and trainers and jockeys and grooms. Cale's eyes were wide as she followed her father down one of the shed rows. She didn't want to miss a thing.

They walked past the stabling area toward the broad, open expanse of the racetrack. Across the dirt oval stood the grandstand, but this time Cale wasn't looking that way. She stood with her father at the rail, drinking in the atmosphere as she watched a handful of horses jog or breeze or work. A slender chestnut caught her eye; the horse's hooves seemed to barely skim the groomed dirt surface of the track as it moved. As Cale watched, the horse's rider turned, spotted them, and waved. Ben waved back.

Cale watched as the horse danced toward them, nostrils flared, ears up, and white socks flashing at the end of long legs. It was the most beautiful horse Cale had ever seen.

Glancing over at her father, she saw that he was watching the lovely chestnut, too. "I like him," Cale commented.

"Her." Ben nodded at his daughter with the hint of a smile. "I like her, too."

Cale felt foolish for not recognizing that the horse was a filly. But she soon forgot about that as her father turned and headed into a nearby training barn. Peeling her gaze away from the chestnut filly, she followed.

Inside they were greeted by a dark-haired man with weathered skin and twinkling eyes, dressed rather surprisingly in nice pants and a brightly striped shirt. As soon as she saw him, Cale couldn't help thinking that he stood out in a barn full of jeans and cowboy hats.

"Balon, you remember Cale?" Ben asked as the man joined them.

Balon smiled at Cale, revealing a flashy gold tooth. "Sure," he said in English flavored with a lively Dominican accent. "She never comes around. She's gotten so big! *Señorita, buenos dias.*"

Cale couldn't answer for a moment. Her attention was fixed on the man's shiny gold tooth.

"That means 'good morning,'" Balon added helpfully.

"Good morning," Cale managed at last. But she still couldn't take her eyes off that gold tooth.

Balon leaned toward her with a conspiratorial gleam in his dark eyes. "I was on a ship coming to America, and a pirate tried to rob me with a gold knife," he whispered. "I bit the knife and it left me with a gold tooth."

He grinned at Cale as she gazed back at him doubtfully. She wasn't sure she believed Balon's story, but she knew it would be impolite to say so.

At that moment there was a flurry of commotion and a clatter of shod hooves from the end of the barn aisle. A second later an enormous black horse plunged into the barn, head high and nostrils flared. Just inside the doorway he suddenly reared, his forelegs pawing the air and his eyes rolling wildly.

Balon grabbed Cale and pulled her into the safety

of an empty stall. Meanwhile Ben moved forward quickly but calmly, grabbing the big colt's reins and pulling him to the ground. The colt resisted for only a moment before he stood still, snorting and blowing. Then Ben leaned down and expertly ran his hands over the horse's lower legs.

"That's the big colt," Balon murmured to Cale as they both watched her father at work. "He's our big horse; his name is Goliath's Boy. You papa feels the legs for heat, make sure the horse is sound. Healthy."

Cale nodded and peered out of the stall at Goliath's Boy. He looked sleek, healthy, and full of energy and spirit — everything a racehorse should be. She watched as her father's fingers probed every inch of the colt's cannon bones, feeling the bones and tendons beneath the animal's dark, glistening hide; then they moved upward to his knees before moving down and finishing their examination with the fetlocks and pasterns.

"You see he's quiet now." Balon nodded toward the colt, who had dropped his head and was standing quietly. "Listening to him. You daddy always say if you listen the horse, he tell you how he's feelin'. . . ."

Cale held her breath, watching every move her father made. She was amazed at his ability to communicate with the high-strung creature as he ran his hands down the colt's legs one last time.

Finally, seeming satisfied, he stood up. "Legs like steel," he said to the groom. "Take him in."

As groom and colt moved off down the aisle, Cale emerged from the stall. As beautiful as Goliath's Boy was, she was relieved to see him go. It was a little scary being so close to a horse like that.

Cale was staring after him when there was a sudden loud snort from immediately behind her. She jumped and spun around — and found herself only inches from a horse's muzzle. It was the chestnut filly she'd seen outside on the track!

Cale froze, and before she could move, the filly snuffled at Cale. Its huge pink tongue flicked out and licked her, and then the horse bobbed its head playfully.

Giggling at the sticky feel of horse slobber on her skin, Cale relaxed. The filly's nose tickled her as it snuffled up and down the front of her jacket before finally focusing its attention on Cale's pocket. The horse nudged her insistently several times.

"What's in your pocket?" Balon asked with a smile.

Cale pulled out a half-eaten package of Twizzlers. The horse grunted approvingly, ears forward and eyes bright and eager.

Balon chuckled. "Sonya likes candy, my friend."

Cale beamed as she pulled the licorice from the plastic wrapping and offered it to the horse. This filly, Sonya, was nothing like Goliath's Boy.

"Sonya," she said, testing the horse's name on her tongue. "Sonya likes Twizzlers."

It was only then that Cale became aware that the filly's exercise rider was still in the saddle. He jumped off and unfastened the girth, pulling the saddle from her back.

On the ground, the young man wasn't much taller than Cale. "Who is this?" he asked in a lilting Cuban accent. "A new jockey?"

Ben stepped forward. "Manolin, this is my daughter, Cale."

Manolin smiled at Cale. "I'm Manolin Vallarta, the greatest jockey in the world," he told her proudly.

Balon laughed. "The fattest jockey in the world," he corrected.

Manolin shot him a dirty look. "Fat?" he exclaimed. "I'm too tall to race. And look at your clothes — this is a barn, not a disco, man!"

Cale smiled. She could tell the two men were joking around.

Then she noticed that her father wasn't joining in the fun. He was examining the filly's legs just as he'd done with the big colt's. But instead of looking pleased, he wore an expression of uncertainty and concern.

Cale felt a flash of worry herself. She knew that a horse's feet and legs were as important as its life's blood —"No foot, no horse," as the old horsemen liked to say. But her attention soon wandered back to Manolin and Balon, who were still poking fun at each other.

If there was anything wrong with Sonya, she was sure her father could fix it.

Chapter 3

Cale spent the rest of the morning hanging out on the backside with Balon and Manolin. There was so much to do and see that she hardly realized her stomach was grumbling hungrily until Manolin pulled out a large cooler filled with sandwiches, cookies, soda, and even pie. Cale ate ravenously, thinking that food had never tasted so good. Everything seemed better at the racetrack!

As the trio finished eating, Balon checked his watch. Cale looked on, mystified, as he stretched out his arms and wiggled his lips around. Then he held up his hands in front of him, pretending to hold something in them. The gold rings on his fingers flashed as he lifted the imaginary object toward his face and took a deep breath . . .

. . . just as a distant bugler began playing the

familiar melody of *Call to the Post*, the signal that called the horses to the starting gate before every race. Cale laughed as Balon "bugled" along. When the bugler finished, Balon swept into a dramatic bow as Cale applauded and Manolin rolled his eyes.

The afternoon's racing had officially begun. A little later, Cale accompanied her two new friends to the paddock, the saddling area where horses were tacked up for each race and allowed to walk around and stretch their legs. That was also where trainers gave jockeys their last-minute instructions along with a leg up, while the betting public could come lean on the fence and check out, in the flesh, the prospects for the coming race. The chestnut filly was scheduled to run next, and Cale didn't want to miss a thing.

They found Ben and Sonya in one of the paddock's saddling stalls. The filly was already wearing the red cotton saddle pad displaying the number 2. Her ears were pinned straight back against her head with unhappiness as Ben crouched beside her, feeling one of her forelegs. A jockey stood nearby wearing racing silks with a matching number 2.

When he glanced up at the newcomers, Ben's forehead was creased with worry. "This leg feels fine," he told Balon, "but she keeps trying to go back to her stall."

Balon gently scratched the filly's nose and murmured

soothingly to her in Spanish. "*Mi novia, la dulcita caballita, venga . . .*" Then he tried to lead her toward the gateway leading out to the track. Sonya took a few steps, then pulled back, shaking her head and snorting.

Ben watched her with a frown. "See?" he said, more to himself than to Balon. "She never does this. She's telling me 'not today.' She wants to go inside."

"Is she going to race today?" Cale asked.

"Of course she's going to race today!"

Cale spun around to see who had answered her question. A man had just entered the paddock. She had never met him before, but she had seen him on TV. He was Everett Palmer, the millionaire international horse trainer who was Ben's boss. Standing beside Palmer was a handsome, well-dressed Middle Eastern man. Several other people hovered nearby.

Her father snapped to attention immediately. "Hello, Mr. Palmer," he said politely. "Nice to see you, wasn't sure you were comin' today." He smiled uncertainly at the second man. "I've never met —"

"Prince Tariq Abal," Palmer interrupted.

Cale stared at Tariq, overwhelmed at the idea of meeting a real, live prince. Tariq glanced briefly at her father, then at her, and nodded regally, seeming uninterested in the whole scene. Then he returned his attention to the horse.

Seeing his client's interest, Palmer grabbed Sonya's lead and gave it a sharp tug. The filly raised her head, standing at attention. The renowned trainer then led the filly in a circle in front of Tariq. "She is as beautiful as she is fast," he announced proudly.

Cale winced as Palmer reached around and gave Sonya a quick swat on the hindquarters. The filly jumped in surprise, prancing nervously as the prince watched.

Palmer handed the lead back to Ben, then turned to Tariq with a big smile. "Sir, I'll meet you in our box seats after I talk to my staff," he suggested.

Palmer waited, his smile never wavering, as Tariq left the paddock with the rest of his entourage. Then he turned to Ben, all traces of the smile gone. "What's the story here?" he snapped.

Her father answered respectfully but bluntly. "I don't think she should run," he said. "She had heat in her right front this morning."

Palmer scowled, then bent to examine the filly himself. He ran two manicured hands up and down her leg, then straightened again.

"I don't feel any heat," he announced. "What did the vet say?"

Ben shrugged. "The state vet and the paddock judge both took a long look and they passed her as fine."

"Good." Palmer's expression cleared instantly. "That's all that matters."

But Ben wasn't finished. "No," he said firmly. "I don't care what they say. I'm saying she shouldn't go today."

Cale couldn't help feeling disappointed as she glanced at the horse standing quietly at her father's shoulder. She'd been looking forward to watching Sonya race. But if her father said the filly shouldn't run, that was good enough for her.

It wasn't good enough for Palmer, though. "Come on, Ben," he said with a sigh, gesturing at the filly. "She's an amazing machine. That's why Prince Tariq paid $750,000 for her."

Cale's eyes widened. *$750,000?* She could barely imagine such a sum.

Seeing her expression, Palmer shot her a phony smile. But Ben had eyes only for his boss — and the horse. "She's not herself," he insisted, "and she doesn't need this. Two of her wins were graded stakes —"

"Prince Abal flew his personal 737 eight thousand miles," Palmer interrupted, sounding irritable now. "For what?"

"To win the Jenson Handi —" Ben began.

Once again, Palmer didn't let him finish. "To beat his brother, Sadir!" he corrected. "Tariq only flies in when he can see one of his horses run against one of his brother's horses." He glanced toward Cale, who was still staring at him. "This is your little girl, isn't it?" he asked Ben.

Cale wasn't sure she liked being called a "little girl." But she kept quiet as Palmer bent down to address her.

"Do you know what a prince is?" he asked with a smile. At Cale's nod, he continued, "They're both princes, Tariq and Sadir, maybe the richest guys in the world. They love to spend millions of dollars trying to beat each other on the racetrack. It keeps *them* angry, keeps *me* rich, and keeps *you* fed."

"She was a champion two-year-old," Ben reminded Palmer. "She's already won both starts this year."

Palmer shrugged. "This will make three for three. She's a little star, no doubt about it."

"She's more than a star," Ben insisted. "I'm tellin' you, she'd do better with some rest."

Palmer's expression darkened. "*You'd* do better by listening to me," he told Ben sternly. "She's a nice horse and I've spent millions of dollars developing a stable of horses for Prince Tariq so that he can beat his brother. I know you've got big plans, but just do your job, okay? Daily maintenance and overseeing the workouts — *your* job. Picking her races? *My* job. You work for *me*."

Cale glanced at her father. Ben's face was red. He nodded shortly at Palmer.

"Great." Palmer immediately sounded as relaxed as ever. "And you do a nice job. Stable looks clean. She looks great." He nodded toward the horse. "Are we good?" At Ben's nod, he smiled. "Good, she's the morning line favorite."

Cale could hardly bear to look at her father now. The humiliation was clear on his face.

"Let's go," Palmer said, glancing around as he noticed Balon and Manolin standing nearby. "Have one of the Mexicans walk her around to settle her." With that, he adjusted his expensive-looking sunglasses and sauntered away.

Cale watched him go, not sure what to think. On the one hand, Palmer seemed smooth and charming. But he'd insulted her father and made him feel like an insect — not to mention calling her new friends "Mexicans" without bothering to notice that neither of them was actually from Mexico. . . .

Ben rubbed his face and glanced at the other two men. "You heard the boss," he said gruffly. "Let's go."

Just then the PA system crackled to life. "Riders up!"

Chapter 4

Ben hardly seemed to remember that Cale was there as he turned to Sonya's jockey. "Nice and easy, okay?" he said. "Don't push early; you know her. Make her settle and then let her unwind at the quarter pole."

The jockey nodded as Ben gave him a leg up. He settled lightly into the tiny racing saddle and bent his knees to tuck his feet into the stirrups.

The filly moved off, prancing a little with nervous energy. Ben strode off toward the tunnel leading to the racetrack, walking so fast that Cale had to hurry to keep up.

The public area of the racetrack was like a whole new world, louder and stranger and more colorful than the backside. Cale stared around at the crowd that had gathered to watch the day's races. Women wearing big, flowery hats and shiny jewelry mixed with tired-looking old men in secondhand clothes who picked through the discarded betting tickets littering the ground. When she looked up at the grandstand, Cale noticed Palmer sitting in one of the roomy box seats overlooking the finish line. Prince Abal and his entourage were also in the box.

Cale's gaze shifted down the row of boxes. In one, well-dressed Japanese men compared notes with each other. Nearby, a group of horsemen in tweeds was also discussing the race. Finally she spotted another wealthy-looking Middle Eastern man around the same age as Tariq. Was that the prince's brother?

Cale wandered up the steps toward the box seats. She wanted to get closer to all those horse people — maybe find out what they were talking about. . . .

A security guard stopped her. "You own a horse, sweetie?"

The patrons in the closest box overheard and turned to look. When they saw Cale, they chuckled and exchanged glances.

Cale felt her cheeks go red. As she realized she'd just made a big mistake, her father appeared and grabbed her by the shoulder. Not saying a word, he led her back down the stairs into the main part of the grandstand. Here the crowd looked a lot less well-heeled than the people in the clubhouse boxes.

Balon and Manolin were waiting for them near a big TV monitor. Balon waved them over.

"There she is," he said when Cale and Ben joined them. He pointed at the TV screen, which showed a close-up view of the horses approaching the starting gate on the other side of the track. "Number two."

Cale looked up and smiled when she spotted Sonya walking toward the starting gate. Forgetting all about the security-guard incident, she focused on the filly as the prerace excitement grabbed her.

"Do you think she'll win?" she asked eagerly.

Balon pulled a slip of paper from his pocket. It was a ticket showing that he'd bet on the race. "I got ten dollars that thinks so," he told Cale confidently.

Manolin reached over and rubbed Cale's head. "For luck," he joked with a wink.

Cale was having a great time. But her father didn't seem to be sharing in the fun. He had pulled out a pair of binoculars and was staring through them in the direction of the starting gate.

Holding her breath, Cale watched nervously as Sonya tossed her head and backed up before stepping forward into her slot in the starting gate. It was almost time. . . .

Just when she thought she couldn't stand the anticipation one second longer, a bell rang and the row of doors in the front of the starting gate sprang open with a clatter. As the horses surged forward, the PA system burst into life, overwhelming even the shouts of the crowd.

"And they're off!" the announcer cried. "Tatler breaks on top with Grand Duke up to join her . . ."

Cale's blue eyes remained fixed on the TV monitor as the horses scrambled through the first furlong of the race, trying to find their stride as they jostled for position. Sonya broke cleanly but not particularly fast. She settled into her stride as most of the others surged forward, her legs flashing steadily and her head pumping in rhythm with her gallop. Her jockey seemed content to hold in eighth as they passed the first pole.

Sonya started moving forward as the rest of the field settled, the adrenaline of the start giving way to the business of running. Her jockey steered her around two slowing horses and took the rail behind the tightly packed leaders.

Cale realized she was bouncing slightly in rhythm to the horse's stride as if she were the one riding the filly. Glancing to the side, she saw that Balon and Manolin were doing the same thing.

"Nice and easy," Balon murmured. "Nice and easy. . . ."

At mid-turn, the two horses in the lead, a big bay and a slender black filly, began to pull away from the field. Sonya's jockey moved her up again, taking her outside around a slowing horse on the rail and into a stalking position in fourth.

"She's fourth!" Manolin cried. "Come on, sweetheart!"

Soon she was third. A few more strides, and she was on the leaders, challenging them as all three raced for the wire. There was less than a furlong to go and the crowd was on its feet, shrieking and cheering and shouting encouragement to their favorites as the three horses battled their way down the homestretch.

Cale hardly heard any of it. Her attention was focused completely on the chestnut filly.

"Go, Sonya!" she cried, her words lost in the roar of the crowd. "Go! Go, baby, go!"

Sonya pulled even with the big bay. The two horses matched strides for a moment, their long legs moving in unison.

Then Sonya suddenly broke stride, the front half of her body abruptly plummeting downward as if she'd just stepped into a hole. She crumpled to the ground, disappearing from the TV monitors. The momentum of the sudden stop sent her jockey sailing through the air. He hit the dirt hard and rolled toward the rail, automatically lifting his arms to protect his head from the thundering hooves bearing down on him as the field passed.

Cale was frozen in place. She stared at the monitor

in shock, not sure what had just happened. The crowd had gone quiet as well; people were groaning and muttering at the terrible sight of a horse down, the finish of the race already forgotten.

Out of the corner of her eye, she saw her father sprinting toward the track. She took off after him despite Manolin's attempt to stop her.

It took Cale a few moments to thread her way through the throngs of spectators and rescue personnel. Finally she reached the scene of the accident. Sonya was on her side, her flanks heaving and her body slick with sweat. The ambulance that always followed the racers around the track was already on the scene and EMTs were tending to the jockey, who was sitting up and clutching his right shoulder.

Meanwhile the equine ambulance had also arrived. A vet kneeled beside Sonya, feeling her right front leg.

Cale stared down at the fallen filly, not sure what to think. Sonya looked scared and distressed. But her eyes were still bright. Maybe she would be okay. . . .

The emergency vet looked up at Ben. "Her cannon bone is fractured."

Ben nodded, his expression grim. He bent to stroke Sonya's nose.

"Okay, sweetheart," he murmured. "It's okay."

Cale heard him and stepped forward. "Is she all right?"

Ben didn't answer or meet her eye. Instead he continued to stare at the filly as the vet crew set up a large white screen around her. When Cale glanced toward the vet, she saw him preparing a large syringe.

She froze with fear. That needle looked like bad news. Why wasn't her father saying anything?

The emergency vet stepped forward, the syringe at the ready. "Ben, I'm really sorry," he said.

Ben finally looked up. When he saw the needle, his face fell and he suddenly looked old and tired. He glanced down at the filly, his hands moving to her injured leg. When he touched it, Sonya let out a strangled yelp of pain.

Cale stared at her father as he let out a choked-sounding cough. He glanced at her, then turned his attention back to the vet.

"Not here, okay?" he said. "Take her back to her stall. . . . Just not here."

The vet looked dubious, but he signaled to his crew. "Sedate her with one cc of detomidine," he instructed.

The equine ambulance backed into position as the vet crew got to work. Cale watched as they gave Sonya a shot and then carefully loaded her into the back of the vehicle.

She looked over at her father, whose face was haggard and worn. Then she glanced up at the sky, suddenly realizing it had started to rain.

Chapter 5

Cale peered into Sonya's stall. The horse was flat out on her side on a bed of clean straw. Whatever had been in that shot had just about knocked her out; she barely seemed aware of her surroundings, let alone her injured leg. Balon and Manolin were standing silently nearby, both of them also watching the filly.

The rain pounded on the barn roof as the vet looked at Cale's father. "Ben, whenever you're ready," he said gently.

Instead of answering, Ben shook his head and scowled. "I can't believe this," he muttered loudly to himself. "I told him —"

"What?"

Everett Palmer had just entered the barn. He was staring steadily at Ben.

"What did you tell me?" Palmer asked as Ben turned to face him.

Ben glared at him. "I warned you that she wasn't sound."

"Ben, you put the saddle on that horse," Palmer reminded him coolly.

"Wait a minute —" Ben protested.

Palmer lifted his hands. "Ben, Ben, Ben. Easy now. It's sad when these things happen in the racing business."

"Business?" Ben repeated.

Palmer shrugged and glanced briefly into the stall. "These are athletes, and this is a business."

"You just knowingly killed a $750,000 athlete." Ben's voice was accusing.

Noticing that Cale was standing nearby watching them, Palmer smiled tightly at her. "Honey, please remind your dad of the first rule of horse racing," he said. "It's not who has the most money; it's who's got the fastest horse."

Ben was getting angrier by the moment. "You pushed her," he spit out. "She was going to be our first Breeders' Cup horse — and you ran her into the ground!"

Palmer raised an eyebrow slightly. "*Our* Breeders' Cup horse?" he said, emphasizing the first word.

"You're forgetting again that you work for me. Ben, our families have known each other for a long time and I gave you a shot to get back on your feet —"

Ben hardly seemed aware of what the other man was saying. "This horse was special —" he began hotly.

"This little girl?" Palmer interrupted. He glanced once again at the filly, who still lay in the stall nearby, motionless except for the slight up-and-down movement of her side as she breathed. "She was a nice horse, Ben, but you're way over the top here."

"Come on, Palmer," Ben protested, surprised out of his anger by the comment. "We were pointing her toward the Breeders' Cup!"

Cale nodded slightly. Only the best of the best, the most accomplished, the greatest and fastest racehorses in the country — the world, even — ran in the eight races that made up Breeders' Cup day. If her father and Palmer had even discussed running Sonya in one of those races, she was more than merely "a nice horse," as Palmer had just called her.

"Maybe I was," Palmer said. "But now she has a broken leg and it's over. Let it go."

Just then Sonya seemed to wake up a little. She thrashed on the ground, squealing in pain as her injured leg moved.

The vet stepped forward, looking concerned. "Ben, we need to make a move here."

But Ben's attention was still on Palmer. "You don't care about anybody," he accused him. "Horses or people!"

"In fact, I do, Ben," Palmer replied. "That's why I'm giving you the opportunity to find a new job."

Ben's jaw dropped. "You're firing me?"

"Yeah, we're done." Palmer waved a dismissive hand toward Balon and Manolin. "Take your Mexicans with you."

That was too much for Ben. He lunged at Palmer, grabbing him by the collar of his expensive-looking suit. Palmer clutched at Ben's shoulders, both men careening into the stable wall.

Balon and Manolin let out shouts of alarm. Balon leaped forward, doing his best to get between Ben and Palmer.

Cale shrank back against the stall wall, terrified. She had never seen her father that angry with someone before. He rarely even raised his voice!

Ben was breathing hard as he stared at Palmer. "You owe me money," he said.

"And you'll get your check at the beginning of the month," Palmer retorted breathlessly, straightening his rumpled clothes.

Ben shook his head. "Pay me *now*," he insisted. "Nine thousand for the last three months."

Cale held her breath as Palmer reached into the pocket of his well-tailored pants. She watched his hand emerge a second later. His fancy wristwatch flashed under the stable lights, distracting her, and it took her a moment to see the huge wad of cash he was gripping. The bills were held together by a gold money clip.

She glanced over at her father, suddenly noticing that he looked as different from Palmer as a hardworking old cart horse would from the sleek Thoroughbreds in this barn. Ben's hands were raw and dirty, his shoes were worn, and his khaki pants were wrinkled and rumpled.

It was strange to think of her father that way, and Cale quickly returned her attention to Palmer. He was peeling bills off the roll of cash.

"Here's six," he told Ben, holding out the money. "Take it or leave it."

Cale stared at the bills. Six thousand dollars! She could hardly believe she was looking at that much money.

But Ben didn't seem pleased. "We agreed on nine," he told Palmer. "You owe me three."

Palmer shrugged. "Then wait for a check."

Sonya was still struggling inside her stall. She let

out another pitiful whinny and kicked out at the stall walls as she rolled over and tried to stand.

Palmer winced, then pointed to the vet. "For the sake of all God's creatures, please, put her down!" he exclaimed.

Cale froze at those words: *Put her down.* She felt tears well up in her eyes. It couldn't be true, could it? Could the beautiful filly's life really be over? She refused to accept that — her mind just couldn't wrap itself around it. She had to talk them out of it, convince them to give Sonya a chance. . . .

"Wait!" Ben said before Cale could speak up. He glanced from Sonya to Palmer. "I'll take the six thousand . . . and the horse."

The barn went silent as everyone present turned to stare at Ben. Even Sonya was quiet for the moment.

Palmer blinked at Ben in obvious surprise. "Six thousand dollars and a dead horse?" he said. "And I never have to hear from you again?"

Ben nodded. "That's right."

"Here's your money."

Palmer handed over the bills he was holding. Then he turned and headed for the exit. Just before leaving the barn, he paused to open his umbrella against the rain still pounding down outside. As he did, he looked back at Ben and Cale.

"It's going to cost you four hundred just to dispose

of the body." He shook his head. "You have a hard head, Ben. Just like your old man. Is he still livin' on that horse farm with no horses? Delusional . . . It's like a disease with you Cranes."

With that, he turned on his heel and disappeared into the rainy afternoon. Cale watched him go, then turned back to her father as she heard him speak to the vet.

"Sedate her," Ben said. Ignoring the vet's look of surprise, he turned to the others. "Balon, hook up the trailer. Cale, get in the truck."

Chapter 6

It wasn't easy, but they got Sonya onto Ben's rusty old horse trailer. The vet had sedated the horse and wrapped her broken leg in an air cast. Sonya made the trip back to the Crane Horse Farm on her side in the back of the trailer.

When they arrived on the farm, it was night. The rain was still falling, but Cale hardly noticed the weather as she climbed out of the truck and stood watching as her father went to the back of the trailer and did his best to soothe Sonya. The sedative had started to wear off and the filly was confused and agitated. Balon and Manolin jumped out of the truck as well and went to help Ben.

"Manolin, go wake the old man," Ben said.

Cale saw Manolin and Balon exchange an anxious glance.

"Tell him it's an emergency," Ben added. "Go!"

Looking reluctant, Manolin headed toward the farm's main house. While he was gone, Ben and Balon unloaded the filly and led her, one careful, limping step at a time, into the barn. Cale did her best to stay out of their way, not wanting to make the filly's life any more difficult at the moment.

When Sonya was settled into one of the box stalls in the barn, Cale timidly moved toward her. The filly's breathing was labored and her eyes clouded as she lay on her side with her broken leg wrapped and stabilized. The horse looked only half-awake, but when she heard Cale approaching she lifted her head and gazed at the girl. Cale returned her look, staring deep into the filly's liquid brown eyes. After a moment, Sonya seemed to relax a little. She lowered her head to the straw again and let out a deep sigh.

The quiet of the barn was broken a moment later by a loud, cranky voice. "What could you two geniuses be calling an emergency at night in the rain?"

Cale recognized her grandfather's voice. When she turned to look, she saw Pop Crane standing in the barn doorway under an umbrella, his thick white hair sticking up in all directions and an overcoat flung on over his pajamas. He surveyed the scene inside the barn.

"This'd better be good," he said. "My goat's gettin' wet."

Pop Crane's constant companion, a billy goat with white whiskers and a shock of white hair atop his head, was standing at the old man's side at the end of a leash. The goat chewed his cud as he surveyed the humans before him.

Pop's sharp eyes found the chestnut filly, her prone form visible through the open door of her stall. "Is this about that horse?"

Ben and Balon exchanged a look. Neither of them answered, but Pop had seen enough. "Good night," he growled, already turning to walk away.

Ben hurried out after him. Cale drifted toward the barn door, wanting to hear what they said to each other. Her father and grandfather didn't get along very well — it had been that way since before she was born. She wasn't sure why, though. In her opinion, they were a lot alike.

"I never ask you for anything," Ben told his father gruffly.

"Yeah, I haven't heard from you in months." Pop Crane rolled his eyes. "That's why your business is so good."

He turned away. But Ben spoke before he could go more than a few steps. "I got a filly in there's got a broken cannon bone."

Cale could see the curiosity in her grandfather's eyes as he turned around. "Thoroughbred?" the old man asked. "Racer?"

Ben nodded. Pop Crane glanced from Ben to Cale and back again.

"Put her down," he said bluntly.

Cale gasped. Just then her mother appeared holding an umbrella. Her pretty face showed concern as she gazed at her husband.

"You guys are soaked," she chided gently. "It's almost midnight. Did you think to eat dinner?"

She swooped toward Cale, wrapping her in a dry jacket. "Mom, I need to help them," Cale protested.

"Sorry, honey, not tonight," her mother replied.

"Don't worry, Cale," Ben said. "I'll take care of her."

Without a word, Lilly pulled Cale under her umbrella and, despite her protests, hurried her toward the carriage house.

Ben and his father were left staring at each other in the rain. Pop Crane seemed ready to head back to his own house with his goat.

"You had that horse that shattered a cannon bone," Ben said to him almost accusingly. "You harnessed it so it couldn't move. The leg healed and the horse was fine."

Pop Crane glanced at him. "That was a long time ago. You were just a boy, Benjamin."

"But it worked."

"He was an old lead pony." Pop Crane shrugged. "He healed just enough to walk around for a few more years before I finally put him down . . . which is what you would do if you had any sense at all."

With that, he turned and walked away, his goat following. Ben watched him go, then turned to Balon and Manolin, who were watching from the shelter of the barn's overhang.

"I may need you guys for a few days," Ben told them.

"I'll show Manny where the bunks are." Balon glanced back into the barn. "You really going to stay with her tonight?"

Ben nodded and headed into the barn without another word.

Chapter 7

The next morning, Cale woke up early and tip-toed out to the barn. The rain had stopped, though the stable yard was still dotted with puddles.

When she reached the barn, all was quiet inside. She made her way along the row of stalls to the last one. Inside, she saw her father sitting in the straw. He was fast asleep, his back against the slatted wooden stall wall. Sonya was asleep, too, stretched out in the straw with her nose resting on Ben's lap.

Cale smiled. Finally she had the time to really look at the horse. She ran her eyes over the filly's body, admiring her glossy coat and sleek, powerful muscles.

Part of the filly's body was lying close to the stall door. Feeling bold, Cale reached through the stall door and gave her a soft pat.

With a snort, the filly's head shot up. Cale jumped, startled. Then she turned and raced out of the barn, wanting to get out of sight before her father woke up, too. She didn't want him to know she'd been there.

Later that morning, Cale emerged from the house to see a strange truck parked in front of the barn. Curious, she hurried over and slipped inside the barn to see what was happening.

Inside, Ben was standing with Doc Fleming, a well-respected local equine vet. The two of them were looking at an X-ray as Balon and Manny stood nearby, watching quietly.

Cale stared at Doc Fleming, transfixed by his large handlebar mustache. Then she blinked and tuned in to what he was saying.

"Spiral fracture of the cannon bone," he was saying.

Ben glanced at the vet. "But it's nondisplaced?"

Cale inched forward as the doctor shook his head. She shifted her gaze to Sonya, who was visible through her stall door.

"She'll never race again," Doc Fleming said.

"But she might walk," Ben replied.

The vet shrugged. "There's a chance. It's up to her. She needs to stay calm. The brace I put on should hold."

"We're going to take it real easy with her," Ben told him.

Doc Fleming nodded. "Let's stay close on this, all right?"

"I will," Ben said. "Thanks, Doc."

As the vet quickly gathered his things and left, Ben seemed lost in thought. He took a few steps toward the barn door, then turned and looked around. He blinked as he finally noticed Cale, Balon, and Manolin staring at him.

"Let's pull all the harness stuff," he told them. "There's straps and a pulley in the tack room."

He headed toward the tack room. After a few steps he noticed that the other two men hadn't moved. He stared at them, though both Balon and Manolin seemed to be trying hard to avoid his gaze as they shifted their feet and looked uncomfortable.

"Ben," Balon said at last. "When Mr. Palmer fired you — fired *us* yesterday, well . . ."

"We all don't have no jobs," Manolin finished for him bluntly.

Cale hadn't really thought about that. She knew her father had been fired, but now she realized that when Palmer had told Ben to take his "Mexicans" with him, it meant Balon and Manolin had been fired, too. No wonder they looked worried.

Ben reached into his pocket and pulled out the wad of cash Palmer had given him the day before.

"Here's a thousand each," he told the two men. "I'm sorry it slipped my mind."

Balon and Manolin took the money, but they both still looked uncomfortable. They exchanged a glance.

"What's wrong?" Ben asked them.

"Well, we train racehorses, right?" Balon said. He glanced toward Sonya. "And she doesn't race no more. So —"

Once again, Manolin broke in to finish for him. "Why are we going to hang around to help you try to get a broken racehorse to walk?"

Balon smacked Manolin, looking embarrassed at his tactless question. But he also glanced at Ben, waiting for his answer.

Ben stared steadily at them. "Do you know who this horse's sire is?" he demanded. "Dreamcatcher. Do you know who that was?"

Balon and Manolin remained silent and still. But Cale heard someone else moving in the doorway. She turned to see her grandfather enter the barn.

"Pop, who was Dreamcatcher?" she asked him.

Pop Crane walked over to Sonya's stall. "Won the Dubai World Cup in '96," he answered gruffly. "Won seven of eleven graded stakes and over three million dollars."

Balon and Manolin were still staring blankly at Ben.

"She was a star at the track," he told them, gesturing toward Sonya. "If we can get her to heal enough to breed her to a decent stud we can sell that yearling for, I dunno . . ."

Pop Crane shrugged and scratched his whiskers. "If it's a colt with good conformation?" he said. "Maybe three hundred."

"Three hundred *thousand*," Ben clarified, still staring at Balon and Manolin. "Would you guys like a piece of three hundred thousand dollars?"

Balon smiled. Manolin smiled and whacked Balon. Cale smiled, too. She could tell that they finally understood the plan now. She did, too. "Maybe five hundred thousand," she suggested eagerly, stepping toward the two men.

Manolin grinned at her. "Or nine hundred!"

Cale noticed that her father wasn't smiling. He looked somber and anxious as he looked from the three of them to Sonya and back again.

But Cale herself couldn't help a rush of excitement as she thought about what they were doing. She couldn't wait!

Chapter 8

Over the next few days, Cale put all her extra energy into helping her father and the others take care of Sonya.

She observed carefully as Balon expertly wrapped the filly's injured leg. She watched as Ben and Manolin strung a pulley system from a beam over Sonya's stall, then wrapped a leather sling around the filly's torso. The three men pulled on the pulley rope, helping Sonya struggle to her feet. Cale watched, her heart in her throat, as the beautiful chestnut lurched and threw up her head, her eyes rolling. The men pulled with all their might, grunting and sweating, putting every last bit of muscle into lifting the thousand-pound animal to her feet.

And finally — she was standing! But the men kept pulling until, finally, the filly was suspended in the air, with no weight on her legs. She panted slightly, her nostrils flaring.

Ben, Balon, and Manolin collapsed in exhaustion. They stared at Sonya floating before them.

Just then, Pop Crane walked into the barn, a half-eaten sandwich in his hand. He smiled at Cale, offering her the remaining half, which she accepted hungrily.

Then Pop Crane walked over to the stall to take a look. Noting the three exhausted men, he nodded a quick hello before turning his attention to their handi-work. Cale munched on the sandwich as she glanced from her father to her grandfather, trying to figure out what they were thinking. It was always hard to tell. She decided not to worry about it for now. For now, it was enough that Sonya was calm and content.

The next day, Cale ran to the barn as soon as she got home from school. The soft strains of a Spanish love song drifted from the radio, but there was no sign of Ben or the other men, so she headed straight for Sonya's stall.

The filly was resting in her sling, looking tired but alert. When Cale climbed the gate for a better view, Sonya turned to sniff at her. Cale leaned forward, giggling as the horse's velvety nose tickled her face and neck. Then she leaned forward a little more, trying to stretch in far enough to scratch Sonya on the back.

THUD!

Cale slipped and fell, landing with a grunt. Sonya tossed up her head, startled, and tried to spin around to face the scary noise. But the harness restricted her movement, and she let out a cry of terror at finding herself trapped.

There was the sound of running footsteps. Seconds later Balon and Ben appeared. They were just in time to see Cale struggle to her feet, staring wide-eyed at the thrashing, panicky horse just inches from her.

Ben yanked open the gate and grabbed Cale, pulling her out of the stall. "She's not a pet, Cale," he said sternly. "She's what I do for work now, so you gotta leave her be. Okay?"

Gasping for breath, Cale nodded. "I'm sorry."

Ben's face softened slightly. "It's all right," he said. "We just gotta give her some time."

Cale nodded again, fighting back tears. Sonya was so sweet most of the time — it was scary and disorienting to see that she could panic so easily, becoming dangerous to herself and others just like that wild black colt she'd seen at the track. She would have to remember that from now on. She walked slowly toward the barn door, taking deep breaths to try to keep the tears inside. Finally she couldn't resist a look back over her shoulder. Sonya had calmed down and was craning her neck over the gate, staring after her with soft eyes.

Cale smiled. The filly seemed to smile back, bobbing her head up and down.

And suddenly, just like that, Cale didn't feel like crying anymore.

Later, Cale sat at the dinner table with her mother, laughing and talking. Ben hadn't come in yet, but Cale didn't think much of that. He was so busy these days taking care of Sonya that he often forgot to eat.

Finally he entered, looking exhausted. He was holding a letter in one hand.

Lilly looked up at him with concern. "Let me fix you a plate," she said, already rising.

Ben pulled out a chair and sat down heavily in his spot across from Cale. He opened the letter he was holding and scanned it, his mouth a thin, somber line in his tired face. Cale stared at him silently, not sure what to say.

Her mother broke the silence. "Cale, you want to tell your dad what you were thinking today?" she suggested as she set a plate of food in front of Ben.

"Well, I was thinking," Cale began shyly. "Pop kind of looks like his goat. Have you noticed that?"

Her father nodded, his mouth full of food. He swallowed, but still didn't say anything.

When he finally spoke, it was to Lilly. "How many days they give you at the diner?"

"Monday, Wednesday, Friday," Lilly replied. "But I could take more."

Ben stared down at his food. "Palmer's been calling around," he said. "I can't get any work right now."

Lilly glanced over at Cale. "Okay, young lady," she said, her voice kind but no-nonsense. "You want to go brush your teeth and get in bed? I'll come up in a minute and turn off your lights."

Cale wanted to stay and hear what they were talking about, but she knew better than to disobey her mother. She stood up and gave Lilly a quick hug and kiss. Then she took a step toward her father. But he looked so grim that she stopped short, feeling uncertain.

"Give your dad a kiss," Lilly urged her.

Cale stepped toward Ben. Leaning forward, she waited as he gave her a quick peck.

"Good night," he said.

After Cale had disappeared upstairs, Ben stood and walked over to the sink.

Lilly watched him, her eyes wistful. "You used to stand in this kitchen with your coffee cup in one hand and that girl in the other," she reminded him softly. "You'd rock her for hours."

Ben stared out the window. His gaze fell on the brightly colored real-estate sign in the yard.

"I gotta take down that sign," he muttered.

"The real-estate sign?"

"It's all been sold . . . and we got our first letter about foreclosure." Ben's gaze wandered briefly to the letter on the table. "The only land left to sell we're sittin' on."

Lilly's face blanched. "How much is Sonya worth?"

Ben shrugged. "Nothing unless she's healthy enough to breed."

Chapter 9

Cale sat up in bed, listening hard. The house was silent. Even the usual creaks and groans of the old beams and floorboards were still for the moment.

She climbed out of bed and headed for the window. As usual, she was taking the quiet route downstairs. Otherwise the squeaky old treads of the stairs would give her away in a second.

Climbing out the window, she made her way to the end of the roof and slid over the edge, holding on to the gutter. She took a deep breath and let go, flopping down into the hay pile on the ground below.

Then she sneaked back into the house through the back door. Hurrying to the refrigerator, she opened the freezer door and quietly rustled around inside, emerging with two small packages in her hand.

She let herself out the back door again, being

careful not to make a sound. Still clad in her pajamas, she raced into the dark, silent barn.

When she peeked into Sonya's stall, all Cale could see at first was an enormous chestnut butt. There was a snort as Sonya lifted her head and pointed her ears back toward Cale. The filly's sharp ears could hear the visitor, even if she couldn't see her.

Cale found her way to Sonya's front end. Unwrapping one of the little packages she'd brought, she held it up. It was a cherry Popsicle. After taking a quick lick, Cale held it through the slats of the stall.

She waited. A moment later, she felt a tug. When she pulled back her arm, the Popsicle was completely gone, leaving her with only the stick.

Cale smiled, then repeated her actions with the second Popsicle. When Sonya had finished that one, too, Cale planted both sticks in the ground along the wall of the barn. This had become a nightly routine for girl and horse, and there were already several other sticks standing there.

Whispering a soft good night, Cale headed back inside to bed.

Cale perched on the top slat of Sonya's stall, smiling down at her father, who was humming as he massaged the filly's injured leg. Ben pulled a towel from the bucket of hot water beside him, applying a heat wrap.

The steam rose lazily into the air, catching the beams of bright sunlight that penetrated into the barn. It was a warm day, hinting at the long, hot Kentucky summer to come.

Soon Balon joined Ben in the stall. The two men exchanged a nervous look.

"Okay, Sonya," Ben said quietly, letting go of the filly's leg. "Nice and easy."

Cale leaned forward slightly, holding her breath. She watched, not daring to blink, as the horse tentatively put down her hoof and straightened her leg, putting her weight on it for the first time in weeks.

"That's my girl," Ben murmured. "It's okay." He glanced at Balon and Cale. "She can stand. Not for long, but she can stand."

Cale let out her breath and smiled. She could stand! Sonya could stand!

Cale stared out the classroom window at the beautiful spring day outside, but she wasn't really seeing it. She was lost in her own thoughts.

"Cale Crane," her teacher's voice interrupted the daydream. "Are you working on our creative writing assignment?"

Cale snapped back to attention. "Yes, ma'am."

The teacher gazed at her skeptically. "What's your story about?"

Cale thought fast. "It's about a king . . . and his castle . . . and a magic horse."

She smiled as the rest of the class lifted their heads to listen. Maybe she'd just made up that story this minute. But she liked the sound of it.

Cale carefully entered Sonya's dark stall. The filly was waiting for her. She nuzzled Cale's shoulder as the girl reached into the pocket of her pajamas.

Cale unwrapped the filly's treat. She smiled as she felt Sonya slurp the Popsicle from the stick in her hand.

When the treat was gone, Cale bent down to plant the Popsicle stick in the ground. After many weeks of this little nighttime ritual, the little wooden sticks nearly circled the entire wall.

Cale looked at them, still smiling. Soon she would have to start another row.

Cale sat at a table in the diner where her mother worked, finishing the last few bites of a slice of pie. It tasted great. She licked her lips and glanced over at Lilly, who was counting her tips.

"You make all that money *and* you get to eat as much pie as you want?" Cale said.

Lilly smiled at her. "You can't find a better job."

Cale smiled back. Then her thoughts wandered

back to her favorite subject. "Manny's going to take me to watch him ride a racehorse," she said excitedly. "And then tonight I'm going to muck out Sonya's stall — I'm thinking about painting it."

"It's nice to have a horse around," Lilly commented.

Cale nodded. "Especially after Dad said, 'There will never be another horse on this farm as long as I live. . . .'"

Lilly looked up at her sharply. "Pop tell you that?" she asked. "Don't listen to everything Pop says. Two sides to every story."

"Pop says Dad is the best horseman he's ever known," Cale told her mother. "Said he has a gift."

"Well, that's true," Lilly replied. "We all know that's true. . . ." She fell silent, and her eyes took on a distant expression.

Cale watched her mother, wondering what she was thinking about. Then she took another bite of pie.

Cale leaned on the rail watching as Manolin rode toward her on a lean, shiny racehorse. He had just finished exercising the horse, putting it through its morning workout on the track.

Manolin hopped off when he reached the break, handing over his mount to the groom who was waiting to walk the horse around the shed row to cool it down after its exercise. As the hotwalker moved off with the horse in tow, Cale smiled at Manolin. She thought he looked very handsome in his boots, helmet, protective vest, and riding pants.

"Hello, *señorita*," Manolin greeted her. "*¿Como esta?*"

"Good." Cale was picking up a little Spanish from spending so much time with Manolin and Balon. "Nice boots."

"I exercise a few horses for a couple of owners," Manolin told her. "Little extra *dinero*, ya know?"

Cale nodded, remembering that *dinero* meant "money." Manolin had removed his helmet, and she reached for it. He handed it to her.

"Do you ever ride in races?" she asked him.

Manolin glanced at the ground. "A couple of times I did, but no more."

"Why not?"

"I have bad dreams."

Cale stared at him, not really understanding what he meant. All of a sudden he didn't seem like the happy, smiling Manolin she knew.

"Three years ago," he went on, "I got my first real race. I ran fifth."

"What was the name of the horse?" Cale asked.

"Downtown Swing," Manolin told her. He sighed. "It was amazing."

"Did you ride him again?"

Manolin nodded slowly. "In our second race I was flying into the first turn and I looked under my arm to see if I was clear on the rail." He lifted his arm and glanced under his armpit to demonstrate. "As I looked back up, there was a horse swerving into me . . . my left foot came out of the iron. I slipped to the ground and got run over by three horses. I broke both shoulders, my sternum, and four ribs."

Cale's eyes widened. As she thought about what Manolin had just said, he pulled off his shirt, revealing the potbelly Balon always teased him about. It also revealed several large, ugly scars that crisscrossed his torso. Cale stared at them, awestruck by the sight.

"Punctured a lung, too," Manolin added.

"You never raced again?" Cale asked.

"At night I fall asleep and I'm dreaming I'm in a race on a very fast horse," he said. "I look down, my left foot slips out of the iron, and I begin to fall. Before I hit the ground I wake up wet with sweat."

Cale shook her head, still not quite understanding. "But you still exercise racehorses."

Manolin shrugged. "Just me and the horse alone on the track. Free, no one to bother us. It's much better that way."

Cale couldn't seem to stop staring at the scars, tracing them with her eyes. She noticed that Manolin looked a little embarrassed.

"I'm sorry about your nightmares, Manny," she told him.

"It's okay," he said softly. "It's God's way of telling me, 'No more racing.'"

Chapter 10

Cale walked into the barn. It was late, and she knew her mother would come find her soon and chase her to bed. But she wanted to check on Sonya first.

When she arrived at the stall, the first thing Cale saw was Sonya's harness hanging over the side. Moving closer, she realized that her father was in the stall with the horse. He was slowly rubbing and stretching the filly's injured leg.

As Cale stood there watching, Ben glanced up and spotted her. He didn't say anything, quickly returning his attention to the horse.

Feeling unwelcome, Cale turned and headed for the door. But her father's voice stopped her. "Cale, grab those two brushes."

Turning around again, Cale saw a wire brush and a currycomb sitting on the wall. She grabbed them and walked to the stall door. Ben gestured for her to come inside. Then he took the wire brush, leaving the curry to Cale.

Suddenly, Cale felt a lot more welcome. In the still of the night, it seemed as if she and her father were the only two people awake in the world. She touched the rubber curry to Sonya's chestnut coat, rubbing it tentatively.

"Pop said this farm used to be beautiful," she said shyly after a moment.

"Make small circles," Ben directed her gruffly.

Cale followed his instructions, moving the curry-comb in small circles on the horse's side. For a second, she thought he wasn't going to respond to what she'd said. But then he spoke again.

"This farm *was* beautiful," he said. "Two hundred acres, one of the nicest in Versailles."

He fell silent again. For a long moment, Cale focused on her work, rubbing the curry against Sonya's side and hindquarters, doing her best to bring the dust out of her shiny coat.

Then Ben continued, "Pop owned some really nice race mares. Big, beautiful, female horses."

Cale nodded. She had heard her grandfather talk about the mares many times. "Waveland, Blue Jezebel, and Miss Moffett," she recited.

Ben glanced at her in surprise. "That's right."

"Every year, he'd breed his mares to the best stallions in town and get them in foal and we'd raise the babies on the farm for a year and then sell them at the Keeneland yearling select sale. Like what you're doing with Sonya's foal."

Ben blinked, a bit taken aback. "Pretty much, that's right."

"Pop said he built these stalls and filled 'em with horses." Cale paused in her currying just long enough to indicate the barn around them.

"He made a good living selling yearlings," Ben agreed.

"But you wanted to keep the yearlings and race them, right?"

Ben shrugged. "It was hard watching horses born on this farm go on to win big races."

"So you got Pop to keep a couple of yearlings so you could train them and race them?"

Ben glanced at her sharply. "Why are you asking me all this if you already know it?"

Cale could tell she'd upset him. Walking over to the wall, she set down the curry. Then she started for the door. Maybe it would be better if she headed inside to bed.

"Did he tell you about Chief's Crown?"

Cale glanced over her shoulder. Her father didn't seem annoyed anymore. She drifted back into the stall, waiting for him to go on.

"Chief's Crown was born in that stall right there." Ben waved one arm toward a nearby stall. "I told my father, 'This is him.' He was big, even as a baby."

"Chief's Crown won the first Breeders' Cup Juvenile," Cale remembered.

Ben nodded. "And he ran third in the Derby. He went on to make millions on the track and in the breeding shed."

"Chief's Crown," Cale repeated slowly. She'd had no idea such a famous racehorse had been born right there on their little farm.

"Pop sold him," Ben said shortly.

Cale sighed, still imagining what it must have been like to have Chief's Crown right there in the barn. "Would've been nice to have a horse like that."

"Nice?" Ben shook his head ruefully. "You'd never have to work a day in your life. Just take one big horse."

Cale was still thinking about the things her grandfather had told her. "You tried to find that horse. . . ."

"I spent a lot of money trying to find that horse," Ben said with a sigh. "A lot of money."

"Pop said you almost pulled it off."

Ben glanced at her, once again looking surprised.

"Well, I didn't," he said. "We had to sell off all the horses. We started selling off land on the farm."

"You lost all his money."

"Most of it," Ben admitted with a grimace.

"And because of that you won't teach me about horses?" Cale said.

Her father frowned at her. "What do you want to know, Cale?" he asked sharply.

This time, Cale didn't back down. "I want to know why I live on a horse farm with no horses," she said. "Why you and Pop don't talk. I'm eleven, but you two act like it!"

"You want in this business?" her father demanded.

"Yeah." Cale met his stare and held it defiantly.

"Well, all I can tell you is counting on luck to pay your bills is not a way to live your life."

Cale thought about that for a second. "Is Pop still mad at you for losing his money?"

"It was a long time ago," Ben replied with a sigh. "We got through it." He gazed at Cale somberly. "You understand what I did was risky?"

"Yeah." Cale gazed back at him. "And it sounds like fun." She turned and walked away, leaving her father staring after her.

Chapter 11

Cale sat bolt upright in bed, her heart thumping. She had just been ripped out of a deep sleep by the terrified scream of a horse. Thunder rumbled outside, and she could hear sheets of rain slashing against the roof of the house. Glancing at the window, she could see the glow of the coming dawn on the horizon.

Moments later, she was dressed and letting herself into the barn. Her father, Balon, and Manolin were all inside, looking exhausted. Sonya was spinning in her barn aisle, her eyes rolling in her head with panic over the storm. She let out another loud scream, plunging and spooking wildly.

"The storm's easing up," Balon said breathlessly.

Manolin sidled toward the terrified filly. "*Mi dulcita*," he murmured soothingly. "*Caballita . . .*"

Sonya calmed down a little. She stood quietly as

Manolin approached. But as soon as he clipped a lead rope to her halter, she panicked again, rearing and spinning around.

Manolin jumped away, getting clear of the panicked filly's deadly hooves. Once again, the horse was a whirlwind of frenzied motion, her fear turning her into a terrifying creature.

Just then Ben spotted Cale. He motioned for her to leave quietly. Cale gazed at him, puzzled by what he was telling her.

"She'll hurt you, Cale," Ben hissed. "Just leave before she sees you!"

Sonya jumped at the sound of his voice, spinning around in the aisle. Balon dove into a stall for safety, pulling the door shut behind him. Ben and Manolin both moved back out of range as Sonya continued to whip around violently.

Cale's heart was in her throat as she watched the filly. What if Sonya hurt herself again?

"Sonya!" she called out.

Sonya spun around in response and plunged toward her, nostrils wide and eyes rimmed with white. The three men all started forward, screaming to try to distract the manic horse.

But suddenly Sonya stopped. Her entire body seemed to droop as the tension left her. She stepped quietly toward Cale, her hooves clip-clopping on the aisle floor. Cale lifted her hand to take the lead rope, then turned and headed out of the barn. Sonya lowered her head and followed her like a well-trained dog at the end of a leash.

Ben stared, and Balon and Manolin exchanged shocked looks. All three of them followed the girl and the filly out into the stableyard, emerging just in time to see Sonya nuzzle Cale's shoulder gently.

Later, Cale stood close to Sonya's side as the filly picked bits of hay out of a hay net on her stall door. Doc Fleming had just finished examining the filly. He stepped back to join Ben, Manolin, and Balon, who were watching from nearby.

"I'll do her bloodwork," the vet said. "But I don't see why she can't breed. I'll see you on Friday."

Ben exhaled loudly as Balon whacked Cale happily on the back.

"You helped her, Cale!" Balon cried. "She's gonna have a baby! *Yesss!*"

Cale grinned as Manolin let out a whoop. Ben shook Doc Fleming's hand, looking as happy as Cale could remember seeing him.

"I gotta go call in a favor," Ben said, turning to head outside.

Cale followed her father outside and saw that he was heading for his truck. She stayed a few feet behind him. "So, where you going?" she asked, trying to sound nonchalant.

Ben stopped and looked back at her. "Uh . . . goin' to see an old friend." He started walking again.

So did Cale. She stayed a few feet behind him as he neared the old truck. "About a stud for Sonya?" she asked at last.

Once again he stopped and turned. "Yeah," he said, gazing at her. "About a stud." He continued on toward his truck. When he reached it, Cale was still right behind him.

He stared at her for a moment. "You wanna come?" he asked at last.

Cale tried to act casual, taking a moment as if carefully considering the proposal. Finally she shrugged. "Um . . . yeah," she said. "Okay. I'll come."

Ben nodded and opened the passenger door for her. Cale hopped in, trying not to let her excitement show.

Soon Ben's old pickup was trundling up the long, carefully groomed driveway of Ashford Stud. Cale stared out the window, not wanting to miss a thing. She had passed *by* Ashford's gates countless times, but this was her first time passing *through* them. The vast grounds within were breathtaking — two thousand acres of perfectly groomed land and immaculately maintained buildings.

Ben parked in the lot, where his old truck stuck

out like a sore thumb among the expensive vehicles parked there. Cale quickly spotted the barn ahead of them. It was a majestic building, many times larger than her little house and barn put together.

She followed her father inside. The interior of the barn was just as beautiful as the outside, with its clean-swept aisle and roomy oak stalls. Cale read each of the gleaming brass nameplates on the stall doors as she passed.

"Look," she told her father eagerly. "It's Thunder Gulch — he won the Kentucky Derby. Giant's Causeway — he and Tiznow battled to the finish in the Breeders' Cup Class. This is Johannesburg — he won the Breeders' Cup Juvenile."

Ben glanced down at her, clearly surprised by her knowledge. "You learn all that from Pop, too?"

Cale grinned, not revealing her source. Just then a smiling man in his fifties appeared in the aisle. "Hey, Bill," Ben called as the man hurried toward them. "Nice to see you. This is my daughter, Cale."

Bill shook both their hands. "Nice to meet you, Cale," he said, his eyes friendly and kind. Then he turned his attention back to her father. "So, Ben, you call me two months ago tellin' me you got this race mare that needs to be covered, you need a favor . . . then I don't hear from you!"

"Sorry," Ben said sheepishly. "It's been a long road with this filly, but she's ready to go. You going to be able to help me out?"

Bill's smile in response lit up his whole face and made his eyes twinkle. Cale glanced up at her father. She could tell this was going to be good. Her father returned her glance, looking equally excited.

"Right over here . . . " Bill said. "You ready for the world's greatest stud? Okay, Too — bring him out!"

Cale and Ben turned around to watch as a tall, thin man led out . . . a tiny Shetland pony! The pony was shorter than Cale, with a thick mane that nearly reached the ground.

"Wait," Cale said, confused. "That's not — what is that?"

She noticed that her father and Bill were exchanging an amused grin. "This here's Thunder Pants," Bill told her.

"Cale, Thunder Pants is a teaser pony," her father added. "He's going to help Sonya get ready to go into the breeding shed with the stallion."

Cale nodded. Before she could finish processing the information, there was the roar of a stallion from somewhere nearby.

"Okay, Cale," Bill said. "You want to meet the stallion I picked for you?"

The wide door along the back wall opened. Cale's eyes widened as she saw the dark bay stallion standing there, his regal head held high. His muscles rippled and gleamed in the midday sun, and a breeze ruffled his thick black mane.

Bill smiled at her expression of awe. "Cale, meet Grand Slam."

Cale could hardly believe her ears. Grand Slam? Could that really be one of Thoroughbred racing's top sires standing before her? Winner of the Champagne Stakes, second in the Breeders' Cup Spring . . . sire of too many stakes winners to remember . . . she couldn't wait to tell her grandfather she'd seen the great horse in person.

Meanwhile her father was staring at Bill in shock. "Bill, you got me Grand Slam?" he exclaimed.

"Everyone at Ashford has a lot of respect for your family," Bill replied. "I explained your situation and they want to do you the favor of a lifetime."

Ben opened his mouth, but for a long moment nothing came out. Finally he cleared his throat. "I don't know what to say. . . ."

"Just say that you'll have your filly here the first week in May," Bill said.

Ben smiled. "You got it, Bill!"

"That week is the only shot you get," Bill warned.

"He's booked till next year. And you gotta send me half of the fifteen thousand by the end of the week."

The number dragged Cale's attention away from admiring the horse. Fifteen thousand? She glanced at her father, whose smile had faded.

"Fifteen thousand?" Ben repeated.

Bill shrugged. "Grand Slam's normal stud fee is a lot more. We're waiving that completely. The fifteen doesn't even cover our costs and insurance."

Ben looked crushed. "No. I — it's an amazing offer, but maybe I could give you guys a share in the foal to cover any costs."

Bill's face had fallen, too. "We just don't do that," he said slowly, sounding sympathetic. "Not in a case like this. Are you saying that we should call it off?"

Cale held her breath. She could tell that things were suddenly going bad, and it made her sad — especially when she looked at Grand Slam. He and Sonya would make such a beautiful foal together. . . .

Her father's voice was dull. "I'm saying I don't have the money."

"I'm sorry, Ben," Bill said quietly. "I didn't really understand your situation."

"It's okay," Ben replied, already sounding resigned. "I appreciate the try. I'll call you."

Cale was heartbroken as she followed him out of

the barn. She'd always known that her family didn't have much money — that was why they'd had to sell off parts of the farm. But until now, she hadn't understood just how poor they were. Everything her father wanted was back in that barn . . . and he couldn't have it. Watching his back as he walked out into the Kentucky sunshine, she suddenly wanted to cry.

Chapter 12

Cale rested her chin in her hands as she watched her grandfather work his way through his second piece of pie. They were sitting at the kitchen table in Pop Crane's house talking about Cale's day. Pop's goat was nearby, relaxing and chewing his cud.

"I've never seen Grand Slam up close," Pop commented through a mouthful of pie.

"He's got muscles everywhere," Cale said, thinking back to her view of the stunning stallion.

"What did he say?" Pop asked her.

Cale shot him a confused glance. "He's a horse."

"I know." Pop gazed at her. "What did he say?"

Cale caught on. Remembering something her grandfather had told her, she spoke confidently: "He said, 'I am a great champion; when I ran the ground shook and the sky opened and mere mortals parted . . . parted . . . " She searched for the words in her mind.

Pop helped her out. "'. . . the way to victory,'" he continued, "'and I met my owner in the winner's circle . . .'"

Cale picked up the rest. "'. . . where he put a blanket of flowers on my back,'" she finished with a smile.

Pop laughed. "You remembered that," he said. "'Sport of Kings,' you know that? They call horse racing the 'Sport of Kings'?"

Cale could see the wistfulness in her grandfather's eyes. "You ever going to take me to the races?" she asked him.

"I don't go anymore." Pop shook his head. "Haven't been in years."

Cale nodded, hiding a sigh. She had tried. Standing up to leave, she reached for a newspaper and magazine lying on the table. "I can take the *Racing Form* and *Bloodhorse*, right?"

"Your dad doesn't want me teachin' you about horses."

"So I should leave 'em?" Cale asked with a flash of disappointment.

"You should stuff 'em under your shirt."

Cale smiled and headed for the door. She had been talking to Pop for a long time, and she knew her mother would be looking for her soon.

"Cale," her grandfather's voice stopped her, "in that cabinet above the sink . . ."

Glancing at him curiously, Cale headed for the cabinet. She opened it and looked inside.

"Is there a coffee can?" Pop asked.

Cale couldn't see the whole cabinet. She climbed up onto the counter, perching there on her knees. "Yeah," she said, spotting a coffee can on one of the shelves.

"Bring it to your dad, wouldya?"

Cale grabbed the can. She had no idea why her grandfather was sending her father a can of coffee, but she didn't bother to ask. If she hurried home, she might still have time to dash out to the barn to visit with Sonya and read the *Racing Form* and the *Bloodhorse* before bedtime.

"Okay," she promised. "Good night."

Ben was standing by the sink drinking coffee when Cale entered the kitchen. She walked to the table and set down the coffee can.

"Pop wanted me to give you this coffee," she said. Spotting the chocolate cake on the counter, she quickly cut herself a piece. "I'm going to eat my dessert in the barn." She hustled out the door before he could stop her.

She was halfway to the barn, her cake plate balanced carefully in her hands, when she heard a door slam. Stopping, she glanced back toward the house just as another door slammed.

At that moment Ben was storming into his father's kitchen. He slammed the coffee can down onto the table in front of the old man.

"What is this?" he demanded angrily.

Pop glanced up. "A coffee can?"

"I won't take it."

Pop shrugged. "Sorry, it's the only flavor I got."

Ben picked up the old can, pulled off the plastic top, and dumped the contents onto the table. Crumpled bills spilled out, forming a large green pile.

"That's almost twenty thousand dollars!" Ben exclaimed.

His father didn't budge or respond. Instead he continued to gaze at the napkin he'd been writing on with a stubby pencil when Ben entered.

"You watched me sell off this farm bit by bit until there was nothing," Ben said through gritted teeth. "Why're you doin' this?"

This time Pop answered him. "Heck if I know."

Ben headed for the door, leaving the spilled money lying on the table. Before he got there, his father spoke up again.

"Breed the horse," Pop said, softly but firmly. "Pickin' up that filly was the first gutsy thing I've seen you do in years."

Ben turned to face him. "Don't talk to me about guts. I took the biggest swing I could, and I struck out."

"And you gave up!"

Ben spread his hands hopelessly. "I'm broke, Pop. What do you expect me to do?"

"I expect you to take that money, trust your instincts, and breed that horse."

"You told me to put her down!"

"But you didn't, did you?" his father retorted. "No — because you're a horseman, Ben. Are you going to spend your life shovelin' pies for sheiks, or are you going to get back in the game?"

"No," Ben cut him off before he could go on. "I got a kid now. I'm done with all that."

Walking back to the table, he quickly stuffed the money back in the coffee can. He stared at the old man for a long moment. Then he picked up the can and headed for the door.

"And don't think I don't see what's goin' on here with you and Cale," he said.

His father glanced up, his expression startled and a little guilty. "Cale's a beautiful kid, Ben —"

"And I don't want this life for her," Ben broke in firmly. "So stop filling her head with horse stories."

"Horse stories are all I got!"

"Good, keep 'em to yourself." Ben reached for the door. "I'll pay you back when the foal sells."

He left. Pop sat there for a moment. Then his face broke into a smile. He glanced at his goat.

"See how easy that was?" he commented contentedly.

Cale looked up from giving Sonya a hug to see her father entering the barn. She was thinking about the baby the filly might have soon — whether or not the Grand Slam plan worked out.

"Any chance you'll keep the foal?" she asked her father eagerly. "Race him? Or her?"

Ben shook his head. "No, I gotta sell the foal," he said gently. "But we'll still have Sonador."

Cale blinked at him, confused. "Sonya door?"

"That's Sonya's full name," her father explained with a slight smile. "Sonador."

"Sonador," Cale repeated, rolling the name around on her tongue to try it out for size. She decided she liked it. It sounded exotic.

"It's Spanish," Ben told her. "It means 'dreamer.'"

Cale glanced at Sonya thoughtfully. Yes, the name definitely suited her.

"Good night, Dreamer," she whispered, giving the filly one last scratch before heading inside to bed.

Chapter 13

Cale was in the barn with Manolin when she heard the clatter of a truck coming into the yard. She raced for the door. Doc Fleming was supposed to come by that day to give Sonya her final checkup before she went over to Ashford for her breeding to Grand Slam. Cale still wasn't sure where her father had gotten the fifteen thousand dollars to make it happen, but she didn't really care. All that mattered was that their dreams were about to come true — soon Sonya would be in foal to the glorious stallion, and then all they had to do was wait for the foal to be born and all their troubles would be over.

"Come on," she called to Manny.

The two of them skidded out into the sunshine. Balon and Ben came hurrying out of the house as the vet's truck came to a stop in front of the barn. Sonya stood in her paddock chewing a mouthful of grass and watching all the humans curiously.

Balon and Manolin were grinning from ear to ear as the vet climbed out of his truck. "Doc Fleming, we gonna be rich!" Balon crowed happily.

"All of us," Manolin added. He jabbed a finger toward the filly. "This horse, she gonna make a special baby."

Ben stepped forward with a smile. "Doc, she's gonna breed to Grand Slam," he said, the enthusiasm plain in his voice. "Don't ask me how I did it. . . ."

He fell silent as the vet stood there, not returning any of their smiles. There was a moment of silence. Finally, Doc Fleming spoke, seeming to choose his words carefully.

"The test results came back," he said to Ben. "I'm really sorry, guys."

Ben shook his head, the smile replaced by a look of bewilderment. "What?"

The vet took a deep breath. "She's infertile."

Cale blinked, not quite understanding. She watched her father wave one hand weakly, then walk away, speechless.

"So she's not going to have a baby now?" she asked the vet.

Doc Fleming shook his head sadly. "She's never going to have babies."

Manolin and Balon looked just as shocked and devastated as Ben. They both walked away, their faces grim. Ben paused in front of the paddock, staring at the grazing filly. Then he strode away.

Only Cale remained in the yard. She walked over to Sonya, staring at her with disbelief. All their dreams, over just like that. . . . The filly lifted her head, her eyes seeming worried.

Cale tried to find a way to comfort her. "It's okay, Sonya," she murmured. She hugged the filly tightly, trying to stop the tears that were threatening to spill over. "It's okay."

Chapter 14

Very early the next morning, as Cale crawled out of bed for her daily visit to Sonya, she heard voices in the kitchen. Curious, she tiptoed to the stairs. They creaked as she crept down, but her parents didn't seem to hear her. Their voices were raised and frustrated.

"It's almost dawn," Lilly was saying to Ben, as Cale came into earshot and froze, listening. "You've been up all night."

"What was I thinking, Lil?" Ben cried, pacing back and forth. "Tryin' to breed that horse . . ."

"Cale loves that horse."

Ben grimaced. "That little filly just ruined me."

"That little filly is the best thing that ever happened around here," Lilly countered. "Since she's been in that barn we've had a family for the first time in years. I'll work seven days a week at the diner if it means you'll spend time with your daughter."

Both of them went silent, staring at each other. Cale held her breath, afraid they'd turn and see her watching.

Finally Lilly spoke again, staring at Ben with both pain and sympathy in her eyes. "Just because your father disappointed you, doesn't mean you have to disappoint Cale."

"This has nothing to do with my father," Ben muttered.

"This has *everything* to do with your father."

Ben shook his head. "You're wrong. The truth is, if Cale hadn't been with me that night, I would've left that horse on the track . . . let them put her down. And I'd still have my job!"

Cale gasped, drawing her mother's attention. When Lilly gestured toward the stairs, Ben turned and saw her, too.

"Cale . . ." he began.

But Cale didn't want to hear what he had to say. Glaring at him, she raced back upstairs.

In her room again, she locked the door and started stuffing a few important belongings into her backpack — some clothes, a book, her favorite hat, a pack of gum. Both her parents came to her door, gently knocking and calling to her. But she ignored them.

She pulled on her boots and headed for the window. Months of sneaking out over the roof every night to go visit Sonya had given her plenty of practice, and a moment later she was free.

Dawn was breaking as Cale crossed the yard and entered the barn. Sonya looked up with pricked ears as Cale approached her stall, already sensing that something was different today.

Entering the stall, Cale bent down to examine the filly's legs. Just as she'd seen her father do so many times, she started with the hinds, running her hands over hock and cannon with long, sweeping strokes.

Then she moved to the forelegs. She removed the wrap from Sonya's injured leg and carefully felt it. Bone, tendon, and muscle felt cool and strong beneath her hands.

Wiping away a few stray tears, Cale looked up at the horse. "Okay, girl," she said. "Let's go for a walk."

Leaving the horse for a moment, Cale went to the tack room and picked out a bridle that looked as if it would fit. She carried it back to the stall and tried it on, gently sliding the metal bit into Sonya's mouth and buckling the throatlatch and noseband. The leather was a bit stiff from disuse, but Cale hardly noticed.

She led Sonya out of the stall and down the aisle. Now all she needed was a saddle. . . .

Sonya stood patiently as Cale hoisted a pad and

saddle onto her back, then carefully buckled the girth, pulling it snug around the filly's barrel. Next, Cale pulled down the stirrups and adjusted their length.

Finally, everything was done. It was time.

Cale led Sonya close to the edge of the nearest stall. Wearing her backpack over both shoulders, she climbed up the gate and, not giving herself a chance to think about what she was doing, slid over into the saddle.

Holding her breath, Cale waited to see what the filly would do. It felt strange being on a horse that might only have three good legs. But Sonya remained calm, seeming unperturbed by Cale's weight on her back.

"Okay, Sonador," Cale murmured. "We're just going to walk — nice and easy. . . ."

She nudged the filly with her legs, and Sonya took a few steps forward. Her ears twitched curiously as she stepped out of the barn into the cool dawn air. Cale was so focused on the horse beneath her that she didn't notice that her father was walking across the yard with a coffee cup in his hand. Not until she heard his panicky yelp —

"Cale!"

Ben dropped his coffee, startled by the sight of the horse and rider. Lunging forward, he made a grab for Sonya's reins.

But the filly had other ideas. Dodging his hands

with a snort, she leaped forward, heading straight down the driveway.

Cale could do nothing but hold on, the reins flapping uselessly just out of her reach. The horse accelerated quickly into a brisk canter as she flew out the end of the drive onto the dirt road that ran the length of the property. Then her ears pricked forward and her stride flattened out into a gallop. For the first time in four months, Sonya was doing what she'd been bred to do — run.

Her arms wrapped around the filly's neck, Cale struggled to stay on. Her backpack had slipped, dangling off one arm and threatening to unbalance her. She buried her face in Sonya's mane, praying for the filly to stop.

Sonya hardly seemed aware of the girl on her back. Her nostrils flared to scoop in the cool morning air, and her eyes gleamed with exhilaration. There were no other horses to race, and so she raced the wind, the air, the dawn. She ran for the joy of running, the blood of a thousand generations of racers pounding in her veins.

Over the rhythmic pounding of hooves, Cale became vaguely aware of another sound approaching from behind: an engine. Her father was racing after them in his truck, his foot pressed down on the accelerator as he chased the runaway horse.

Finally he caught up, pulling alongside Sonya and then passing her. He skidded to a stop about an eighth of a mile ahead and jumped out, waving his arms and shouting Cale's name.

Cale managed to lift her head. She saw her father standing there waving to her. Sitting up in the saddle as best she could, she flung off her backpack. As Sonya neared Ben, Cale began to lean toward him.

As the filly thundered past, Ben reached up and grabbed Cale from the saddle. The momentum flung him backward and he clung to her as they both tumbled into the ditch beside the road.

When the dust cleared, Ben and Cale sat up and looked at each other, breathless and coated in dirt. Cale's heart was racing, and she could hear her father gasping for breath.

"You okay?" Ben wheezed. "Cale?"

Cale nodded, and closed her eyes as he grabbed her into a tight hug. She hugged him back, feeling numb after what had just happened.

"It's okay, Cale," Ben murmured soothingly. "It's okay. . . ."

A moment later pounding footsteps caught up to them. Balon and Manolin had seen what was happening and followed the truck on foot.

"Go get Sonya," Ben told them. "Take the truck."

The two men jumped into the truck and took off

in a squeal of tires and a spray of dirt. Ben stood, with Cale still clinging to him, and headed back toward the farm.

Lilly met them on the road, her arms outstretched and her face drawn with worry. But Ben waved her off, still holding Cale tight.

"We're okay," he said gruffly.

Chapter 15

A little while later, Cale was eating a piece of pie in the kitchen while Ben watched her. There was a knock on the door, and Balon and Manolin entered.

Manolin looked uncharacteristically serious, and Cale's heart skipped a beat. "*Señor* Crane, can we talk to you?" he asked. "Outside?"

Ben rose and followed the other men through the door. Cale jumped to her feet. She was sure they were going to talk about Sonya — was she okay? Had that wild run hurt her, reinjuring her leg?

She headed outside, where the men were already talking.

"She ran up and down the fence," Balon was saying. "We were riding next to her, in your truck —"

"Is she hurt?" Ben interrupted anxiously. "Did she break down?"

Cale joined them, looking from one serious face to the next. She wanted to hear the answer to her father's question, and she also didn't want to hear it. If Sonya was hurt, it was all her fault. . . .

"In the truck we see that it's about a quarter mile," Manolin said. "And, well, she . . ."

"She kept getting faster," Balon finished.

Ben's face relaxed into a smile. Then he laughed with relief. Cale didn't quite understand; she moved a little closer to Balon, hoping he would explain.

"She looked strong, sir," Manolin said.

Ben was still grinning. "Are you saying she should race?" He laughed, louder and longer than Cale had heard in a long time.

She stared at him. What was so funny? This sounded like good news. Sonya was okay! She had healed; her leg was just as good as new!

Ben stopped laughing when he realized nobody was joining him. He stared at Balon.

"The last time was about twenty-three seconds," Balon said. "At least maybe the doc he can look and see maybe it's okay."

Ben nodded thoughtfully. "We'll talk in the morning."

"Who's Mariah's Storm?" Cale asked curiously.

It was the next morning, and she was perched on

Cale Crane lives on a horse farm
with no horses.

Manolin and Balon quickly
become Cale's new friends.

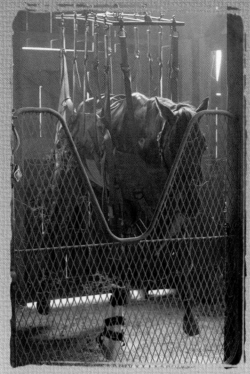

When Sonya is injured in a race, the Cranes decide to help her.

Cale sneaks out of her room to go to the barn.

Cale shares her ice pops with
the injured Thoroughbred.

She's sure that Sonya can race again.

Cale and her father begin training Sonya together.

Cale believes Sonya can win the Breeders' Cup Classic.

Cale rejects an offer of $100,000 to buy Sonya.

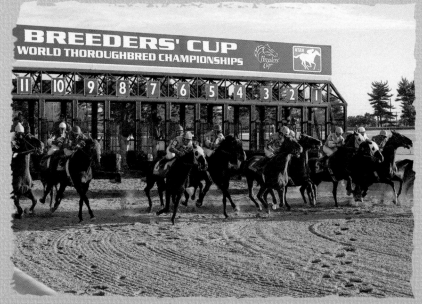

And they're off!

Sonya makes her move.

Cale and her father enjoy Sonya's victory.

In the winner's circle, the Cranes
and their friends celebrate.

Cale and Sonya prove that dreams can come true.

the paddock fence eating a piece of toast. Doc Fleming was there, finishing his examination of Sonya. The vet had just mentioned a horse called Mariah's Storm to her father, who looked rather stunned.

"Mariah's Storm," Ben repeated. "She's the dam of Giant's Causeway. She broke her leg in the same way as Sonya and she came back to race?" He glanced at the vet as he asked the question.

Doc Fleming nodded. "She came back and beat Serena's Song in a graded stakes," he replied.

Ben was silent for a moment, taking that in. Then he scowled at the vet.

"And you didn't think to tell me about Mariah's Storm the first time you saw Sonya's leg?" he demanded.

Doc Fleming shrugged. "For every Mariah's Storm there are hundreds of horses that never make it."

Ben sighed. "My dad always says God put horses on earth to keep men humble."

"Smart man." Doc Fleming smiled. After a moment he glanced over at Sonya. "But she's doing really well. I'm very happy."

"What should I do?" Ben asked him.

Cale held her breath, waiting for the answer. She glanced at the vet.

"You're the horseman, Ben," Doc Fleming replied. "Only you and she know what's right."

In the following weeks, Cale tried not to think too much about the future. Instead she spent every moment she could with Sonya. The pair became such fast friends that before long the filly was following Cale everywhere — even to the bus stop. Cale even helped exercise the filly by running in circles around a tree in the front yard so that Sonya would jog after her. Girl and horse also took long walks through the fields near the house and spent hours together in the barn and paddock, communicating without words. In the meantime, Cale paid close attention to everything her father did as he carefully conditioned the horse on the lunge line and on the road. She knew he was using all the knowledge and horse sense he'd gained over a lifetime to help Sonya's injured body heal clean and strong.

More than a month after the vet's last visit, Cale watched steam rise from Sonya's sweaty body as Balon hotwalked her after her latest workout. She filled a water bucket at the barn's spigot, preparing to sponge off the filly. Meanwhile her father just stood there staring at the stopwatch in his hand, mulling over whatever it was telling him.

Pop wandered over to join him. Ben kept his gaze on the watch as he spoke to his father. "In five weeks, the best she's done is three furlongs in 37 seconds."

Ben glanced at his father. "You think that's fast enough?"

Pop knew that Ben already knew the answer. But he responded anyway. "For a cheap claimer at Bluegrass Downs," he said bluntly.

Ben sighed and glanced at the watch. "She was a graded-stakes horse, now she's a claimer."

"You don't think anyone would claim her?" Pop asked.

"Would you buy a horse who broke down in her last race?" Ben glanced at Sonya, speaking now to himself as much as to his father. "Question is, can she beat fifteen-thousand-dollar claimers?"

"And they're off!" the announcer howled over the clang of the starting buzzer.

Eight horses lunged out of the starting gate in a perfect line. Cale leaped onto the bench where her mother was sitting, standing on tiptoes for a better view. The track at Bluegrass Downs was much smaller than the big oval at the fairgrounds, and several sets of its rickety, two-hundred-foot, metal bleachers could have fit inside the bigger track's grandstand.

But Cale wasn't paying attention to such details at the moment. She was too busy watching Sonya. The filly had broken well and was on the rail running third at the moment.

"She's third, but there's a pack coming," Cale reported to her mother.

She watched as a cluster of four leaders raced into the turn. Sonya fell behind them, now lying fifth. Cale noticed that the filly hadn't yet changed her lead — was she still favoring her injured leg more than they'd thought?

"Only three furlongs to go," she muttered.

Another horse passed Sonya on the outside. Cale could see the chestnut filly's jockey urging her to keep going. The leaders were right in front of them, blocking their way. He steered her to the outside as the field entered the homestretch. Soon she passed one horse, moving back into fourth . . .

Cale hopped up and down, making the bleachers shake. Lilly stood, caught up in the excitement of the stretch run.

"C'mon, Sonador!" Cale yelled. "Every step!"

Sonya surged forward, passing another horse. There were only two ahead of her, in front by several lengths. Stride by stride, Sonya gained on them . . . step by step . . .

The horses flashed under the finish line. The race was over. Sonya had come in third.

Cale cheered wildly, then raced down the bleachers with her mother following. A few minutes later she found Sonya in the race barn. The filly's sides were heaving and her eyes were still flashing from the excitement of the race.

"Way to go, Sonya!" Cale cried, rushing forward to give the horse a hug. "Third place! What does she get for third?" She turned to her father questioningly.

"Eleven hundred dollars," Ben replied, with a disappointed glance at his wife, who had just followed Cale into the barn.

Balon was listening. "One minute thirteen seconds is a little slow," he said. "But it's a start, my friends!"

Cale smiled. She knew that Balon was right. This was Sonya's first race back — she was only getting started!

As they all chatted about the race, a short, stern-looking man approached their little group. He was carrying a stack of envelopes and checking the numbers on the stalls he passed.

"Sonador — Ben Crane?" he inquired, stopping in front of Sonya's stall.

Ben nodded. Cale stepped out of the stall, gazing curiously at the stranger.

The man handed Ben an envelope. "Claimed," he said.

Ben stared at the envelope in utter shock. "You gotta be kiddin' me," he said. "No way!"

"Claimed?" Cale repeated. "What's he talking about?"

"Get in the truck," her father replied gruffly. "C'mon. Let's go."

Cale stared after her father as he walked away. "You think I don't know what a claiming race is?" she cried after him. "I can't believe you really did this. You never said it was a claiming race!"

She couldn't believe this was happening. In a claiming race, every horse was for sale — anyone with a trainer's or owner's license could file a claim to buy any of the entries up until post time. After the race, the new owner paid the stated fee and took possession of the horse.

"What was the tag?" she demanded as her father stopped and faced her. "How much?"

"Fifteen thousand," Ben replied wearily.

Cale's jaw dropped. Fifteen thousand dollars . . . "You just sold Sonador."

Ben's face was haggard as he stared at her. He opened his mouth, clearly struggling to find the words to explain.

But Cale didn't want to hear it. Spinning on her heel, she raced away as fast as she could.

Chapter 16

Later that night, Ben found Cale in Sonya's empty stall. He opened the door and leaned against it, waiting for her to look up.

When she didn't, he spoke anyway. "I wasn't trying to sell Sonya," he said quietly. "Out of a hundred horses that could've been claimed tonight, do you know how many got claimed? Two."

Cale still didn't look at him. She stared at the straw on the stall floor, struggling to keep from crying. She'd cried enough already.

"There was no chance someone was going to claim a filly with a broken leg," Ben went on.

Cale couldn't resist that one. "Well, I guess there was some chance," she mumbled. "'Cause she's gone."

"Well, that's my luck." Ben sighed. "She was a good horse. I miss her, too, Cale, but —"

"Don't treat me like a little kid," Cale interrupted. She stood up and wiped her face on her sleeve. "You were trying to get some of your money back. I get it. It's a business."

"That's right. It's a business."

Cale glared at him. "And you're bad at it."

"I won't deny it," Ben said. "But I wasn't trying to sell her."

"You lied to me!" Cale said fiercely. "You said I'd always have Sonador. You stood right there and said it!"

"I said we weren't going to keep the foal," Ben corrected. "It's a tough game. We're not raising pets."

Cale clenched her fists. "You raced her, and she got claimed!" she cried accusingly.

Ben took a step toward her, but Cale backed away. "Welcome to the world of horse racing," he said, losing his patience a little. "You want to be in the business? Well, things change."

"She wasn't for sale!"

"Every racehorse in the world is for sale," Ben retorted. "Get that."

Cale shook her head, anger bubbling up inside her. She'd had enough of her father's excuses.

"She was my horse," she spat out. "And you know it!" Pushing past him, she sprinted out of the barn.

*   *   *

The next day was Parents' Night at Cale's school. Lilly was working at the diner, which meant Ben had to go alone. He already felt uncomfortable as he entered the school; Cale was still angry with him. How could he make her understand that he hadn't meant to let Sonya get claimed? He wasn't sure.

He felt even less comfortable when he saw all the parents sitting at their children's desks in Cale's classroom.

A teacher stepped forward to greet him. "Hello. And you are . . . ?"

"Ben Crane."

The teacher smiled. "Cale's father, great! Here's a name tag. Parents are sitting at their child's desk to get a feel for the school day."

Ben did his best to smile at the teacher. Then he went and wedged himself behind Cale's desk.

He spent the next half hour or so staring out the window and trying to stay awake. The other parents were talking, asking questions, and reading stories their kids had written. But Ben was hardly paying attention. He wasn't even sure why he was here. He'd learned more about his daughter from watching her in Sonya's stall or at the racetrack than he ever could by being here. . . .

"Ben Crane?"

The teacher's voice snapped him out of his daydreams. "Yes, ma'am," he responded, sitting up as straight as he could in the too-small desk chair.

"I'd love you to read a bit of Cale's story," the teacher suggested cheerfully. "It's very inventive."

Ben felt his cheeks flush as the other parents turned to stare at him. He wanted to get up, make an excuse, and leave. But he couldn't. Cale was already mad at him — how much angrier would she be if he embarrassed her at her school?

Ben moved to the front of the classroom and picked up the essay the teacher set before him. He cleared his throat.

"'Once upon a time,'" he began, reading as quickly as he could to get it over with, "'there was a noble king. He lived in a beautiful castle overlooking green fields. An evil storm cast darkness over his castle, and before he knew it, dark knights had begun to take away his kingdom, one piece at a time.'"

Ben paused and gulped. Something about this story was starting to seem familiar. . . .

Reading a little more slowly, he continued. "'But our king was a warrior, and he knew that if he could find his magic horse, he could restore the kingdom to greatness. He was not like most kings . . . he was quiet and kind. Everyone loved the king, which he may not have known. He searched and searched, and finally rescued his horse from a raging river.'"

He stopped again, taking a deep breath. He could feel the other parents' eyes upon him, but he didn't care.

"'But by the time he'd freed his horse,'" he went on, his voice now clear and slow, "'his kingdom was gone and he had given up. But the horse knew better than he. The horse took him over mountain ranges and across raging rivers. When it finally looked like they would die, the horse asked him to trust him. The king didn't know if the horse had really spoken to him or if he just hadn't had anything to eat in a few days. Not long after, the horse attempted to climb a mountain so steep that the king was sure it would be their deaths. But the horse reached the top. At the top they found his kingdom restored. All those who loved him greeted the king with pie and coffee.'"

The classroom was silent as Ben finished. He stared down at the paper in his hands. His cheeks were still burning, but this time it was with pride and emotion. He suddenly found himself very glad that he'd come to Parents' Night after all.

Chapter 17

Cale woke up as she felt someone sit down on the edge of her bed. Turning sleepily, she saw that it was her father. He was holding some papers in his hand.

"I read your story tonight at school," he said softly.

Cale pulled the covers over her head, embarrassed. "The stupid one about the king?" she mumbled.

"Yeah, the stupid king."

Cale heard her father exhale loudly. Curious, she pushed the covers away and looked at him. For a second she'd almost forgotten she was mad at him. And now, looking at his tired face, she couldn't quite bring back the anger from before.

"I've made mistakes, Cale," he said heavily. "And I'm sorry."

Cale pushed herself upright. She could see that

her father was struggling to find the words to go on. Maybe she could help him. . . .

"So you like the stupid king?" she asked.

"Yeah," Ben smiled slightly. "I like the stupid king."

Cale gazed at him. "I love the stupid king."

"He loves you, too."

Cale threw her arms around her father. He hugged her back tightly, his arms feeling strong and warm.

When Cale came down to breakfast the next morning, her parents were already in the kitchen. Ben was at the sink drinking coffee, while Lilly bustled around between stove, table, and refrigerator.

Cale flopped down into her seat and yawned, glancing at the window. It was the start of another beautiful day.

"You want pancakes, Cale?" Lilly asked.

Before Cale could answer, the screen door flew open. Pop stomped into the room.

"Ben," he snapped. "There's a guy here to see you."

As Pop disappeared outside, Cale glanced curiously at her father. She got up and headed for the door with Ben right behind her.

Outside, a horse carrier was idling in the driveway. Ben hurried past Cale and handed the driver an envelope. Pop was standing nearby watching the whole scene.

"Cale," Ben said, turning to her. "I got Pop another goat. Would you get it out of the trailer?"

Cale stared at him, puzzled. What did Pop need with a second goat? Was his goat lonely?

But she did as Ben said, heading for the rear of the horse carrier. Using all her weight, she managed to pull open the door. It was dark inside, and after the brightness of the morning sun, she couldn't see much. Then an old goat stepped forward, blinking in the light.

Cale smiled at the goat, watching it step toward the edge of the trailer. Then she heard something else moving inside.

She glanced toward the sound and gasped — a beautiful chestnut filly was stepping toward her! Sonya came forward and nuzzled Cale's shoulder, just like always.

Cale led the filly out. "Sonador!" she cried. "You came home!"

She threw her arms around the filly's neck. Then she led her away from the trailer, still hardly daring to believe her eyes. Sonya sniffed her all over, looking for treats.

After the horse trailer pulled away, Cale danced over to Ben and Pop, leaving Sonya nibbling at the grass. "How'd you get her back?" she demanded happily.

Ben shrugged. "Well, Pop helped, too."

Cale turned and hugged Pop, then ran back to Sonya. Meanwhile, Pop was staring at his son in surprise.

"I did?" he asked. "I helped?"

Ben smiled slightly. "Let's just say, we're out of coffee for a while."

Pop nodded, understanding now. His eyes twinkled, and he turned along with Ben to watch the happy girl and her horse.

That evening, the whole family — Cale, Lilly, Ben, Pop, Manolin, and Balon — gathered in the barnyard for a barbecue. Manolin wielded the barbecue tools like a pro, grilling everyone's food to perfection.

Cale hardly noticed that her father had disappeared for a few minutes before he returned, carrying a file folder.

"Here's all her paperwork," he said, handing the file to Cale along with a pen. "Sign here, please."

Cale glanced at him cautiously as he flipped open the folder and indicated a line on one of the papers. But she did as he said, carefully signing her name, using her best penmanship. She wasn't sure what was going on, and nobody else seemed to know, either. Everyone was staring at them curiously.

Ben smiled at all of them. "I put fifty-one percent

of the horse in her name," he explained. "Cale, you make all the decisions from here out."

Cale gasped in amazement as the others murmured in surprise. Pop was staring at his son.

Ben turned to him. "Don't worry, I gave you thirty-nine percent," he told his father. "Balon and Manny split ten."

"What're you saying?" Balon exclaimed.

"The new owner of Sonador is Cale Crane." He patted Balon on the back. "You work for her now."

Before the others could figure out how to respond, he walked away with a smile.

Chapter 18

The modest dirt oval of the Thoroughbred Training Center seemed to glow in the pink light of dawn. Cale could hardly believe she was here — as Sonya's trainer and owner. She turned to see Balon and Manolin arguing over a bag of breakfast pastries nearby. Balon was holding Sonya's lead. The filly was tacked up and ready to go; Manolin was dressed in boots and a hardhat.

Giving up on the pastries, he turned to Cale for instructions. "You want me to warm her up and then push a little for three furlongs?" he asked. "Or maybe four?"

"You just want to blow her out today?" Balon put in. "And we can start to build her up?"

Cale nodded slowly, trying to decipher what they

were talking about. She decided Balon's suggestion sounded better.

"Yeah," she said. "Let's just blow her out today."

Balon gave Manolin a leg up. Sonya pranced a little as the rider turned her toward the track.

Cale leaned over the rail. She had brought a pair of binoculars and a stopwatch, just like her father always carried. Now she peered out at the track through the binoculars, keeping her eyes trained on Sonya.

As Manolin put the filly through her paces, Cale did her best to keep track, watching the poles as Sonya flashed by them. She checked her stopwatch and jotted down the times confidently. She knew Sonya could do it.

When Cale walked down the stairs to the kitchen that night, carrying Sonya's folder, she overheard her father on the phone. His voice sounded oddly chipper and cheery.

"Well, that's too bad," he was saying. "If anything comes up, you'll let me know? Great. Okay, good night."

He hung up and turned away, his face sagging. When he heard Cale and glanced up, she gazed at him curiously.

"You're up late," he told her.

"Been reading all of Sonador's records." She

glanced down at the folder. "She won over two hundred thousand in graded company."

"I know."

"That qualifies her for a lot of stakes races," Cale went on. "I was looking through the conditions book."

"I'm sure you'll figure it out." Ben sounded a little distracted.

Cale stared at him, willing him to pay attention. This was important. She'd thought long and hard about it, and it was the only way to help Sonya. . . .

"I need you to help me," she blurted out. "I want you to help me train her."

Ben glanced at her, all his attention back on her now. "Oh, yeah?" he said carefully. "What do I get?"

Cale had already anticipated this question. "Ten percent," she replied.

Ben laughed. "Twenty."

"Fifteen," Cale countered.

"Done."

Over the next few weeks, Cale made Ben earn his percentage. He showed her how to examine Sonya's legs for heat or swelling, how to lunge her, how to time her workouts. Cale soaked in all the knowledge like a sponge, always eager to learn more. She watched with pride as Sonya bloomed under their care, her muscles and wind improving every day.

One night over dinner in the kitchen, as the whole gang gathered around the table, talking and laughing and helping themselves to the feast Lilly had prepared, Cale decided it was time for her big announcement. She'd been thinking about it a lot lately, scouring the conditions book that listed all the possible races Sonya might enter. She'd finally made up her mind — and she couldn't wait to tell everyone.

Standing on her chair, Cale called for attention. Everyone slowly settled down and turned to look at her.

"I've scouted all of Sonador's possible races," she said. "And I've picked a race that I know she can win." She waited as the others went silent, staring at her curiously. "Saturday, October 29th," she went on. "I've gotten the best jockey. His name is Manolin Vallarta."

Manolin was in the process of shoveling food into his mouth. He stopped short, glancing up. "Wait," he said. "*My* name is Manolin Vallarta."

Cale smiled at him. "You once told me that you were the greatest jockey in the world. And I believe you."

Manolin looked alarmed as he lowered his fork. "I can't!" he exclaimed. "I'm not ready, I —"

Balon grabbed his plate and fork out of his hands. "Too fat," he scolded. "You need to slim down."

Everyone laughed. Meanwhile, Ben was looking puzzled.

"Cale," he spoke up, "I'm pretty sure October 29th is the day of the Breeders' Cup Championships. I don't really think you want to run in any race the same day as the Breeders' Cup."

Balon, Manolin, and Pop nodded and murmured their agreement. Breeders' Cup Day was a whirlwind of activity, press coverage, and general craziness second only to Kentucky Derby Day. It would be difficult to go about the business of running on such a day — especially with a horse who was really still just starting to get back into racing.

"You're right," Cale told them. "We shouldn't run in any race on the same day as the Breeders' Cup. That's why she's going to run *in* the Breeders' Cup."

There was a moment of dead silence. The adults all exchanged shocked glances.

Ben was the first to speak. "You can't just show up at the Breeders' Cup with your horse and say, I'm here, I wanna run in the Classic," he told Cale, doing his best to keep a straight face.

Cale looked straight at her father.

"The first seven horses get in on points," she said, as Ben nodded. "The last seven they base on points and overall performance during the year. But they do have the ability to make a judgment call." She tilted her chin defiantly. "I'm going to take a shot," she added. "Why not me? Why not Sonador?"

The porch was silent. Nobody seemed to have a response to that.

Finally, Balon spoke up, sounding excited. "We're gonna run in the Breeders' Cup Classic!"

Chapter 19

Cale knew her father still wasn't convinced that her Breeders' Cup dream was going to come true. But he seemed willing to let her try. And she was determined to show him that dreams could come true — if you just believed in them enough.

She spent every moment she could watching Sonya train and learning everything she could about racing. One day at the Thoroughbred Training Center, she stood at the rail beside her father as Manolin and Sonya swept by. Cale clicked her stopwatch and glanced over at Ben.

"Five furlongs in just under a minute," she said.

Ben shrugged. "That's better, but . . ."

"She was breezing, Dad," Cale reminded him. "Don't worry."

Ben smiled. Cale could tell he was impressed by

her growing knowledge of racing lingo. She had learned that breezing was different from galloping which was different from working. There was so much to learn!

Just then, Balon approached, carrying a box of doughnuts. Ben and Cale each grabbed one.

A few minutes later, Manolin led Sonya off the track toward them. His eyes lit up when he saw the doughnuts. "Oooh — breakfast!" he exclaimed. "I'm so hungry."

Before he could reach for a doughnut, Balon handed him a very small orange and a bottle of water. Manolin stared at the orange with obvious dismay.

"You sure this is an orange?" he cried. "Looks like a painted golf ball!"

Cale smiled at him sympathetically. She knew it was hard for him to give up the delicious food he loved, like doughnuts. But he needed to get in shape and lose weight if he was going to be ready to ride Sonya in the big race.

Day after day, the training regimen continued. Ben worked with Sonya carefully, developing her muscles and her mind. He taught her to regulate her stride better, to conserve her speed until the best moment came to use it. He showed Cale how to schedule the horse's workouts to best improve her times. They ran the horse on the dirt track at the training center, but also on the hills and trails around the farm, using the natural undulations of the landscape to strengthen her bones and tendons and balance, and to keep her mind fresh.

And day after day, the filly improved. One day at the training center, Ben clicked his stopwatch as Sonya flew past.

He glanced over at Pop, who had come along that day. "Forty-seven, flat," Ben told him.

Pop didn't answer. But he looked impressed.

The day of the Breeders' Cup selection arrived. Cale, Ben, and Pop were sitting in a noisy room in the Breeders' Cup Headquarters; it was filled with other hopefuls, horsemen of all ages sitting there looking tense as they waited to hear their fate.

Near the front of the room, Cale spotted Everett Palmer. He was standing with Prince Tariq, who smiled as Palmer whispered something in his ear.

Then Cale turned her attention to Prince Tariq's brother, Sadir, who was pleading his case with the Breeders' Cup chairman, an older gentleman dressed in a suit.

"But, sir," Prince Sadir was saying, "my horse, Rapid Cat, is the son of Storm Cat, the best sire in the world. He deserves to run in the Breeders' Cup —"

"Mr. Sadir Abal?" the chairman interrupted. "Wishman Stables? Rapid Cat is eighteenth on the points list. There are fourteen spots. It doesn't look good for Rapid Cat."

There was the sound of meowing as Sadir sat down, looking sad. Cale saw that Palmer and Tariq were the ones making the meowing noises, obviously trying to heckle Sadir.

The crowd in the room moaned and shifted with tension as a woman entered and handed the chairman a file. Cale sat as still as she could, wondering when her turn would come.

"Next," the chairman announced. "Is Mr. Cale Crane here?"

At the sound of her name, Cale jumped to her feet, her heart pounding. "I'm Cale Crane," she announced. "*Ms.* Cale Crane."

Palmer glanced at her with a smirk. "Why don't you stand up?"

The rest of the room burst into laughter. Cale frowned, not amused by the joke. Yes, she was a little younger — and shorter — than the others here. But she deserved to be here just as much as they did.

The chairman glanced down at his paperwork.

"Miss, your horse, Sonador, only has sixteen points, which puts her sixteenth on the list. Though I see that she had forty-two points last year."

"Yes, sir," Cale said. "She'd have that many points this year, only she got injured."

The chairman looked more interested now. "Do you have a vet's report? Says this horse is sound?"

Thanks to her father's advice, Cale was prepared for this. She marched to the front of the room and handed the chairman the report Doc Fleming had typed up about Sonya's health.

The chairman scanned it and nodded. "Fourteen horses get to run," he told Cale. "You've got a shot. But to pre-enter this horse, the fee is forty thousand dollars. Did you bring a check?"

Cale gulped as the room went silent. "I mailed it . . . today," she lied.

Several people laughed. Cale felt her face turning red.

The chairman gazed at her sternly. "Let's just say the panel determines Sonador belongs in this race," he said. "There's another eighty thousand dollars of entry fees due by October ninth. You prepared for that?"

The room was silent. Cale flushed as she felt the eyes of dozens of wealthy owners and trainers fixed on her.

"She'll mail it to you," Palmer joked.

The room erupted in laughter again. Ben started forward, looking angry, but his father held him back.

Cale glared at Palmer, who was laughing. She had never felt so humiliated in her life.

The chairman did his best to hide his own amusement as he spoke again. "Final selection, eleven A.M., Wednesday," he said, dismissing the group.

On Tuesday night, Ben arrived home from picking up Lilly at work to find Cale perched on the top rail of Sonya's stall, lost in thought. The filly stood quietly inside, nosing at her hay.

"You should try to get some sleep," Ben told his daughter. "Big day tomorrow."

Cale nodded. She looked at her father, trying to gauge his mood. He looked happier and more relaxed than usual. She smiled.

"How much you going to bet on Sonador to win the Classic?" she asked him.

Ben hesitated. Cale's smile faded.

"Don't you think she can win?" she demanded. As her father stayed silent, she continued, urgent now, "You gotta think she can win; what's the harm in thinking she can win?"

Ben still didn't have an answer. Cale hopped down from the rail and grinned at him.

"Say, 'I think she can win,'" she ordered.

Finally Ben smiled. He couldn't resist her optimism. "I think she can win."

"Good." Cale nodded. "She needs to hear you say it."

She walked away, leaving her father alone with the horse. Ben turned to see Sonya looking out at him.

"What are you lookin' at?" he asked her gruffly. He reached out and scratched her nose affectionately.

Chapter 20

The next morning, people jostled for position at Breeders' Cup Headquarters as the chairman appeared and took his spot at the front of the room. Cale's heart was pounding so fast she was afraid it would jump right out of her chest. Beside her, her father and grandfather were just as anxious. She stared at the chairman, waiting breathlessly for him to speak.

"As chairman of the Breeders' Cup," he began, "I am proud to announce the field for the twenty-second running of the Breeders' Cup Classic. In alphabetical order — A. P. Flyer . . . Argus . . . Bicycleman . . ."

Cale glanced over and saw Palmer standing nearby, wearing sunglasses and looking smug. He grinned at her when she caught his eye. Beside him, Prince Tariq also looked smug.

Glancing around the room, Cale found Prince Sadir. Unlike his brother, he looked nervous.

The chairman waited for a steward to place the names he'd just called on the large display board at the end of the room. Then he moved on to the next three names on his list.

"Goliath's Boy," he announced. "Hestoomuch . . . Iconduit . . ."

Cale looked up at Pop, who was squinting at the display board. Ben was staring that direction, too, his face white and pinched.

The chairman called three more names, but Cale hardly heard them. She watched the steward place the wooden nameplates next to the corresponding numbers: seven, eight, and nine. That meant there were only five places left. . . .

Three more names. Three more slots filled. The chairman cleared his throat. Cale glanced up at the ceiling and closed her eyes, hardly daring to hope.

"And the last two runners," the chairman said, "are Point Twice and . . . Sonador."

Cale's head snapped back down, and her eyes flew open. Ben looked up from staring at the ground. Pop continued to squint, not quite sure if his ears were failing him.

But Cale was sure. Grabbing Pop, she shook him excitedly. "We got in!" she screamed. "WE GOT IN!"

She turned and scanned the room, her heart pounding with happiness this time instead of nerves. Prince Sadir Abal was shaking his head sadly, and Cale felt a flash of pity. His horse hadn't made the list.

"All outstanding fees must be paid by Wednesday at noon," the chairman reminded the room.

Just then, Cale's eyes found Palmer. She stared at him, grinning proudly. He stared back. Then, after a moment, he turned away and shot a smooth, practiced smile at an approaching reporter.

That night in the Cranes' barn, the radio blared as Cale and her team settled Sonya in for the night. None of them could stop chattering about the exciting news of the day. Cale was so happy she felt as though she might burst. They were in!

Suddenly a voice broke up the party, clear even over the lively song playing on the radio. "I had to see it for myself," Everett Palmer said. "It's amazing."

Cale spun around to see Palmer standing there in his expensive suit, looking as out of place as a billionaire in a soup kitchen. Manolin immediately reached over and turned off the radio, while Ben glared at the unwelcome intruder.

Palmer strolled a little farther into the barn, glancing around with keen interest. "It's good to see all the

Cranes in one spot." He paused, nodding to Manolin and Balon. "Evenin', boys."

Walking over to Sonya's stall, Palmer bent down to feel the filly's legs. Feeling protective, Cale hurried over to stroke the horse's nose reassuringly. Palmer glanced up and smiled at her protectiveness. He stepped back and looked over at Pop.

"Pop Crane," he said. "The famous Pop Crane." He chuckled at the tense, silent faces all around him.

"How can we help you?" Pop asked tightly.

Palmer shrugged. "You have to ask yourselves what it's worth to you to have this broken filly finish four-teenth in a field of fourteen. How much do you really want to embarrass yourselves? Because everyone here knows that this horse has no business in that race."

"Let us worry about that," Pop retorted, his eyes flashing.

"The Breeders' Cup Classic is the richest two minutes in American sport," Palmer went on. "It's the shining face of the entire industry. It needs to remain unblemished."

Cale scowled. "So you're here for the good of the sport?" she challenged him. "I think you're here because you're scared Sonya's going to beat your horse."

"Beat my horse?" Palmer chuckled, then turned to Cale's father. "Honestly, Ben, I feel bad about what happened between us. I'm here to make it right."

Narrowing her eyes at Palmer, Cale waited to hear what he would say next. Everyone else was watching him, too.

"I'll give you twenty thousand in cash for her." Palmer pulled a thick wad of money out of his pocket and held it up, showing them all. His expression was smug as he waited for their response.

A smile played around the corners of Ben's mouth as he glanced around the barn. "Twenty grand," he began slowly. "Let's see, Manny, that's a thousand dollars for you and a thousand dollars for Balon."

Manolin scratched his head. "Gee, a thousand dollars," he said. "I could get a couple of nice steak dinners with that — bring some girls, some wine . . ."

"Thousand dollars for me?" Balon added, gazing wide-eyed at Palmer. "Wow, maybe you throw in those fancy shoes — I really like your shoes."

By now everyone was grinning or chuckling — except Palmer. He scowled at them, seeming a little confused.

"Wait," Pop spoke up. "My share would be almost eight grand. I've only got about twenty grand invested. So I'd be losin' twelve grand! Great deal, where do I sign?"

The room erupted with laughter. Palmer reached into his pocket and pulled out another stack of bills.

"Forty thousand dollars," he said, a hint of

desperation creeping into his voice. "I brought my guys and a trailer with me. It's your lucky day, Ben. Prince Tariq has sent me here on a mission. I know what you paid for this horse. Are we done here?"

The laughter quieted a little. Ben gazed evenly at Palmer.

"She's not my horse anymore," he said.

Palmer looked at him, puzzled. His gaze wandered to Pop, who shook his head. Then Palmer noticed Cale staring him down.

He smiled at her. "What do you say, honey?" He held out the money.

Cale crossed her arms. "I'm not selling."

Palmer laughed, though it sounded a bit forced. "Okay, I found my other pocket." The smile faded from his face. "Listen to me — last chance, kid. I have a certified check for one hundred thousand dollars . . . and if you take this offer, I'll give your dad his job back."

He pulled a check out of his pocket. The room went dead quiet as he held it out toward Cale.

Cale stared at the check for a second, then glanced at the faces around her. It was so quiet in the barn that the soft sounds of Sonya shifting her weight in her stall seemed to echo.

Cale turned to Ben. "Dad?" she asked him uncertainly.

"You want my advice?" Ben asked. When she nodded, he added, "I would tell him to take his money and his empty trailer and get off my farm."

Satisfied, Cale returned her attention to Palmer. "You're running the big colt, Goliath's Boy, in the Classic?" she asked him.

"That's right," Palmer said. "Goliath's Boy is the favorite. And when he wins the Cup he'll be my fifth Horse of the Year."

Cale tilted her head thoughtfully. "Do you think Goliath's Boy remembers what Sonya's butt looks like?"

"Why?" Palmer looked confused.

"'Cause it's all he's gonna see of her on race day."

Laughter rang out through the barn again. Palmer glared at Cale, seeming to loom over her as he pointed one finger in her face.

"You got a real smart mouth, little girl," he hissed furiously. "But you should wise up —"

Before he could finish the threat, Ben leaped forward and slammed him back against the wall. He pulled back his fist, holding it at the ready.

"Don't you ever talk to her like that!" he warned.

Balon jumped in and grabbed Ben before he could hit Palmer, who pulled free. "You're crazy," he spat out, already hurrying toward the door. "Every Crane is crazy!"

Chapter 21

Cale was dumping Sonya's morning grain into her bucket when Manolin came panting up to her. Even though it was a warm, beautiful morning, he was dressed in a hooded sweatshirt, gloves, and snow pants.

"I've lost fifteen pounds in three weeks," he told Cale, jogging in place as he spoke.

"You should stop training." Cale's voice was dull and listless. "We don't have the money to run. I'm going down to tell the Breeders' Cup people that we're dropping out of the race."

Manolin shook his head, still jogging. "No, I had a dream last night that I was on a horse," he said breathlessly. "A fast horse. That horse and me, we were flying like angels."

Cale couldn't help smiling a little at his enthusiasm. "Yeah, Manny? How did it end?"

"I woke up," Manolin said. "My hunger was gone. It was God, telling me to race again. Thank you, Cale. May God bless you."

He jogged away, smiling. Cale watched him go, wondering about what he'd just said. How much could you really believe in a dream anyway? She wasn't sure anymore.

A little later that morning, she was standing in the yard talking it over with Pop. "You never thought she'd get in," she reminded him.

"No, I didn't," he agreed. "But you did it."

Cale nodded. She was still proud of that, no matter what happened next.

"There's other races, Cale," her grandfather reminded her. "Races that don't cost so much to enter."

Just then, Ben hurried up to them. "Get in the truck," he told them briskly. When they just stared at him, not moving, he repeated, "Get in the truck!"

Cale and Pop exchanged a glance and a shrug. Then they did as Ben said and got in the truck.

Soon, the three of them were jostling down the road, the old truck's shocks squeaking all the way. Cale was silent as she looked out the window. She had no idea where they were going, but she knew better than to ask. Her father would let them in on the secret only when he was good and ready.

She realized the truck was approaching the gates of Wishman Stables. Cale's eyes widened as her father stopped in front of the gates and turned to face her.

"He's expecting us," he said.

"Great idea, Dad!" Cale cried. She had just figured out her father's plan. "What are you going to say?"

"I'm not." Ben smiled slightly. "You are."

Cale gulped, suddenly a little less enthusiastic about the plan. But she would do it. She had to — for Sonya.

A pleasant-looking, older Middle Eastern man opened the door at Cale's knock. "I'm here to see Prince Sadir Abal," Cale told him, trying to sound as grown-up as possible.

The man smiled at her. "The prince is expecting you. Please join him."

Cale turned and grinned at her father and grandfather, who were standing behind her on the doorstep.

The man who had answered the door showed Cale to a large, bright room inside the opulent house. There, a group of Middle Eastern men were sitting around a long table breakfasting on yogurt and fruit.

Cale saw Prince Sadir Abal at the head of the table. She entered the room bravely. "Prince Sadir," she said. "I'm Cale Crane."

"I remember you." The prince studied her face solemnly.

"And this is my dad and my grandfather," Cale added, waving toward Ben and Pop. The two of them were standing in the doorway, looking as awkward and uncomfortable as humanly possible.

"Howdy," Ben muttered to the room at large.

"Mornin' to you," Pop added.

It was quiet for a moment. Then the prince smiled.

"Join us," he told the Cranes graciously, gesturing to the breakfast table.

"A filly with a broken leg is going to run in the Breeders' Cup Classic?" one of Prince Sadir's men asked Cale in disbelief.

The men around the table laughed. Cale stared at the remains of the meal they'd just finished, feeling a little sheepish. When he said it that way, it sounded pretty bad. . . .

"Quiet!" Prince Sadir shouted, waving his hand at them. As the group fell silent, he turned to Cale. "That's why you came here?" he asked her. "Cale, you look me in the eye and tell me you think your horse has a chance to beat my brother's horse."

The prince's eyes held no trace of humor now. They were icy cold and serious.

Cale met his stare and held it. "My horse will beat every horse that shows up."

She heard a few gasps and sighs from the other men as they reacted to her confidence. But she kept her gaze trained on the prince.

Prince Sadir nodded thoughtfully. "Tariq is sure he's going to win," he mused. "He has a big, big horse and he always wins!" With that, his icy stare turned into a smile. "What do you need from me?" he asked Cale.

Cale was taken aback by his sudden change of demeanor. She glanced toward her grandfather for help. "Well, I need for . . . " she began tentatively.

"Four million?" Prince Sadir interrupted, turning to snap his fingers. "Get the checkbook!"

Two men jumped up from the table, ready to obey. Cale gulped.

"*Forty thousand,*" she corrected the prince hastily. "Forty thousand dollars for the nomination fee. And eighty thousand for entrance fees."

"Oh, a hundred and twenty thousand," Prince Sadir laughed, then glanced at his men. "Get me cash."

The same two men sprinted out of the room. Cale glanced over at Pop in astonishment.

"This is a gift," Sadir told her. "But if she wins, you pay me back double."

"*When* she wins," Cale corrected him.

Prince Sadir smiled at her confidence. "Goliath's Boy is a very fast horse," he reminded her.

Ben spoke up. "Goliath's Boy is a bully," he said. "And her horse knows it."

"What is the name of this girl, your horse?" Prince Sadir asked.

"Sonador," Cale replied.

Sadir smiled, seeming pleased. "Sonador . . ."

Late that night, Ben pounded on his father's door. "In twenty-one Breeders' Cup Classics, do you know how many fillies have ever won?" he demanded when Pop answered the door.

Pop stared at him. "None," he replied. "Only three fillies have ever run."

He burst out laughing. But Ben remained serious. "So what am I doing?" he exclaimed.

His father stopped laughing. "You're taking your kid and your horse to the Breeders' Cup tomorrow," he replied seriously. "Because that's the dream of every real horseman. . . . It's the dream of every father . . . a dream very few get to see." His voice sounded choked up on the last few words.

Ben gazed at him, surprised at the rare show of emotion.

"Very few," Pop repeated. "Trust me on that."

"Listen," Ben broke in, speaking quickly before he could lose his nerve. "I want you to come to the race."

Pop was clearly taken aback. "You know I don't go to the races anymore," he said, giving Ben a chance to back out of it. "Plus I've got nothing to wear. . . ."

"As your son, I'm asking that you come," Ben said firmly. "And be with me and Cale."

They shared a long look. Then Pop nodded.

"Okay."

Chapter 22

Breeders' Cup Day dawned crisp and breezy over the elegant limestone buildings and beautifully landscaped grounds of Keeneland Racetrack. Horses had been arriving all week long, coming from near and far for the crowning day of the year for Thoroughbred racing.

Cale stared wide-eyed as Pop drove up the track's long drive, which was lined on both sides with a spectacular row of maple trees in blazing fall color. Her eyes next turned to the grandstand ahead, which was already crawling with people. She wondered if Sonya was safely in her stall yet. Her father, Balon, and Manolin had driven the horse to the backside in their trailer, but Ben had insisted that Cale travel with her mother and grandfather.

They parked and climbed out of the truck. As

they entered the track, Cale could almost feel the energy and anticipation all around her. She stared at the colorful crowd in the stands and then out to the quiet expanse of the track. Keeneland was as different from the humble little oval of Bluegrass Downs as the Crane Horse Farm was from Wishman Stables.

The three of them quickly made their way through security and onto the backside. Cale led the way to the barn where Sonya would be spending the hours leading up to the race.

When she entered, she saw her father standing with his back to her in the doorway of Sonya's stall.

"You look *muy bellissimo*," Balon said.

"Thank you," Ben said with a slight laugh.

"I was talking to her."

Balon smiled at Cale, who smiled back shyly. She was dressed up for the occasion, too. So was her mother, who looked youthful and pretty in a purple dress and a fancy new hat Ben had bought for her.

Pop pushed past Cale and into the stall, holding a brown paper bag. "These are the original silks of the Crane Horse Farm," he said, pulling out a silky shirt and holding it up so they could all see.

The shirt's front featured a red circle with an elegant crane in flight. The sleeves were bright green and slightly faded with age, but somehow it all worked together perfectly.

Manolin reached for the shirt, gazing at it reverently. Stripping off his T-shirt, he pulled on the silks.

Cale was surprised when she saw how thin Manolin was when he took off his shirt. She knew he'd been on a strict diet and exercise program, but she hadn't realized just how much weight he'd lost.

Once he was wearing the silks, Manolin seemed to stand a little taller. Ben smiled, then turned to his father.

"Wow, incredible," he said. "Thank you."

Pop seemed a little bit embarrassed, but pleased. "I'm going to take this beautiful woman to the owner's box so she can show off that hat," he announced, offering Lilly his arm. The two of them turned and strolled out of the barn.

The next few hours passed quickly. The barn was swamped with owners, trainers, grooms, reporters, and all sorts of other onlookers. Everywhere she looked, Cale saw wealthy people and beautiful, fit horses. But she had eyes only for Sonya.

Finally it was time to make their way to the paddock to saddle up for the race. Cale was excited enough to burst as she followed the filly beneath the stunning pin oaks and sycamores dotting the picturesque paddock area. Sonya was prancing, her nostrils flaring slightly as if she were scenting the prerace buzz in the air.

The paddock was packed with reporters — every saddling stall had a small entourage in front of it. As they passed Goliath's Boy's spot, Cale noticed Palmer standing out in front of the big colt, holding court for the media.

Just then, Sonya snorted and jumped, then popped up into a slight rear. Cale returned her attention to the filly. "Okay, Sonya," she said soothingly. "Easy now."

Palmer had just spotted them. "Ben Crane and Sonador!" he shouted. "The eighty-to-one shot!"

The reporters surrounding him immediately turned their attention — and their cameras — onto Sonya and her group. The filly froze, her eyes wide with uncertainty as she faced down the cameras.

Ben stepped in front of the horse. "No questions, please," he said gruffly.

"C'mon, Ben," Palmer goaded with a glint in his eye. "How 'bout a shot of Sonya and Goliath's Boy together?"

Before anyone could react, Palmer yanked Goliath's Boy forward, leading him straight toward Sonya. Sonya reeled away, her eyes rolling fearfully. Goliath's Boy arched his neck at her threateningly, baring his teeth and lunging forward.

The crowd shrieked, and people backed away from the two agitated horses. Sonya moved away from the colt so quickly that she slammed into the fence and squealed with pain. Goliath's Boy threw up his head and backed off, and within seconds grooms had leaped forward to separate the two horses.

Ben grabbed Sonya's bridle and hustled her away to a safe distance. Cale followed, scratching the filly's nose when she stopped.

"Okay, Sonya," she said, her voice shaking a little. "It's okay."

"Hold her," Ben told Balon.

As the groom grabbed the filly, Ben bent and began a careful examination of her right front leg. At his sharp intake of breath, Cale leaned down to look, and immediately spotted a bright trickle of blood running down Sonya's leg.

"Manny, get my bag from the stall," Ben called sharply.

As Manolin scurried back to the barn, Balon leaned down, trying to see. "Is she bleeding bad?" he asked Ben.

Ben had already snatched the clean handkerchief out of his breast pocket and was using it to wipe away the blood. He squinted at the cut.

"I don't think the cut is bad," he said.

Cale held her breath, hoping he was right. When Manolin returned with the bag, Ben quickly cleaned and dressed the cut. Then he stood and loosened his tie.

"Well?" Cale asked, her heart in her throat.

"The cut's fine," Ben said. "It's only a scratch."

"Okay, great," Manolin said. "Give me a leg up."

But Ben was bending over the filly's leg again, feeling up and down its length. Balon glanced at him with concern. "What do we do, boss?"

"I don't believe this," Ben muttered. "Now I think I'm feeling heat in that leg. Bring her in here."

He strode into one of the saddling stalls. "Dad, is it too risky?" Cale asked, scurrying after him.

Her father looked irresolute. "What are the chances that she gets a cut on the leg we've been trying to heal for the past six months?" he said. "This is beyond bad luck."

"Just say it, Dad," Cale insisted anxiously. "Should we scratch her?"

"I'm sorry, sir," Balon called from outside the stall. "She won't come in."

Ben and Cale looked out and saw Sonya standing proudly outside. Her ears were pricked in the direction of the track, and she was so still that she might have been a statue.

Ben walked over and grabbed her lead. "Okay, Sonya," he said. "Let's go home."

He tugged on the lead, but stumbled back as the horse remained firmly in place. He glanced at his crew, surprised at the resistance.

"She kicked me when I tried to take her in," Manolin reported.

"She wants to run, Dad," Cale said. "She knows why she's here. You saved her life; she's just returning the favor. She's here to run for you."

Ben glanced from Cale to Sonya. He stared the filly right in the eye.

"She's talkin' to me," he murmured.

"What's she saying, Dad?"

"I dunno . . ." Ben studied the horse for another moment. "Something about the ground shaking and the sky parting."

Cale smiled, remembering her grandfather's words. She gazed at her father. He gazed back at her.

"She wants to run," Ben said.

Chapter 23

Somehow, Cale and Balon fought their way through the crowds to the entrance to the owners' boxes. A guard stopped them there.

"Just for owners, miss," he said.

As several people turned to glance curiously at her, Cale held her head high. "I know," she told the guard proudly. "That would be us."

Cale showed him her badge. The guard stepped back, and she and Balon strolled through the entrance. Soon they were standing in their box with Lilly and Pop.

A few minutes later, as the horses pranced onto the track for the post parade, Ben joined them. As he entered the box, he handed his father a betting ticket. "That's for you," he said.

Pop read the ticket and laughed appreciatively.

Cale glanced over and saw that her father had put $257 on Sonador — to win.

The horses paraded past the stands, drawing scattered cheers and calls. Then they continued on down to the turn, trotting or cantering to warm up their muscles.

After that it was time for them to load into the starting gate. Cale stared at the long metal gate topped with the phrase BREEDERS' CUP: WORLD THOROUGHBRED CHAMPIONSHIPS spelled out in gold uppercase letters on a purple background. A few of the horses were fractious as they waited their turn, sensing the excitement of the day. But the assistant starters worked professionally, loading each horse into the gate one after the other. Through her binoculars, Cale could see that Sonya stepped into her starting stall quietly, giving the assistant starters no trouble at all.

Finally the entire field stood ready in a line inside the gate. There was a moment of breathless silence, and then . . .

The buzzer rang, and the gates clanged open, releasing the horses onto the track in a burst of raw energy. *"They're off!"*

Hooves scrabbled against the dirt, long legs sorted themselves out into a gallop, jockeys shouted encouragement to their mounts . . . and the race was on!

Cale's eager eyes searched out Sonya as the horses sorted themselves out within the first furlong. She spotted Manolin's silks first, then found the filly's chestnut head and hindquarters. Sonya was near the back of the pack, number twelve out of fourteen, loping along easily, about one horse-width off the rail.

Out on the track, Manolin felt pleased with the break and with the way Sonya was settling into her stride. He ran over the instructions his boss had given him just before releasing him for the post parade — *Let Goliath's Boy go*, Ben had told him. *Let him bully the whole field until they give up. Then let her try to reel him in. Slowly, wait until you can't wait anymore and then wait some more.*

Glancing back under his right arm, the jockey saw a horse coming up fast behind them. Content to let it pass for now, he nudged Sonya over toward the rail to give the other horse room.

Then he glanced under his left arm. He froze — there was a horse there, too, right behind them, also surging up fast! Somehow he'd lost count, thinking there was only one runner behind them. Panicking, he swung his whole body to the right, trying to keep Sonya out of the way. As he did, his left foot slipped out of the stirrup iron and he felt himself flying forward. He was going to tumble right off over her right shoulder!

Just as he was about to drop the reins, Sonya suddenly jerked over to the right. The sudden move broke Manolin's momentum and sent him flying right back into the saddle. He grabbed at the pommel to keep from tumbling backward.

In the stands, Ben was watching the whole thing through his binoculars. "My God, Manny," he murmured. "Hang on!"

Manolin righted himself and grabbed the reins, which had slipped away to one side. Then he reached down — carefully, carefully — and slipped the iron over the toe of his left boot.

It was only then that he looked around and realized that Sonya was now at the back of the pack. Two lengths ahead, a few stragglers raced against each other while the leaders surged ahead farther up the track.

For a second, Manolin wondered if he should just pull up — avoid embarrassing himself, the Cranes, and Sonya.

Then the filly put on a burst of speed. Her stride opened up, and within a few jumps she had surged past the stragglers.

Manolin looked ahead, his hopes surging along with the filly's stride. They were in the middle of the turn now, and just ahead he could see a group of five that included most of the favorites; they were stalking the speed horses, who had begun to tire at the front of the field.

Sonya swung to the outside, though Manolin couldn't be sure whether he'd decided to make the move or she had. Either way, they slid past the favorites within several strides, leaving them surprised in Sonya's dust.

At the top of the stretch, Goliath's Boy finally made his move. He swapped leads and shifted smoothly into his next gear, passing horses as if they were standing still. As he thundered down the stretch in full stride, Sonya slipped neatly into his wake, taking advantage of the holes he found between the horses in front.

In the Crane box, Balon whipped off his hat. "C'MON, SONYA!" he shouted. "YOU CAN DO IT!"

Cale was jumping up and down, hardly believing what she was watching. Nearby, her father and grandfather grinned at each other, years of defeat and hard luck dropping away and leaving their faces as joyful as Cale's.

With fifty yards to go, Goliath's Boy pulled away from the field and slid over onto the rail. For the moment, his jockey seemed unaware of the chestnut filly stalking just behind him.

But Sonya was still creeping forward. Swinging wide, she put her head at Goliath's Boy's hindquarters. Another two jumps, and she was beside him.

Manolin grinned as he urged her forward. The filly responded, moving even faster as she put her head in front.

The colt's jockey went for the whip, trying to get more speed out of his mount. But it was no use. Sonya grabbed hungrily for the next stride, and the next, and the one after that. Thirty yards to go, and she was a length ahead. Another stride, and another . . .

They flashed under the wire all alone, and the crowd went wild. Sonador had done it! She had just won the Classic!

Chapter 24

"Sonador! Sonador! Sonador!" the track announcer howled. "She's been called the three-legged filly! She just shocked the world at odds of eighty-to-one!"

Cale flung herself at her father, wrapping her arms around his neck. He hugged her tight, grinning with joy. Lilly rushed over and planted a big kiss on his lips. Nearby, Pop was staring at his winning ticket and laughing. Balon quietly crossed himself, then let out a loud yelp of joy: "AAAAAAAAAAAAAH!"

Meanwhile, out of the track, a breathless Manolin had slowed Sonya to a jog. As they made their way back along the track, a reporter on horseback approached with a cameraman on another horse right behind her. The reporter steered her mount alongside Sonya as they all headed toward the winner's circle.

"When did you think you had a chance?" she asked, holding a microphone toward him.

Manolin took off his goggles. He was weeping with joy.

"It was the dream," he gasped out happily. "I had a dream. I never knew the end before today."

They had arrived at the winner's circle, and the reporter peeled off as Manolin rode inside. Through the chaotic crowd, he saw Ben and Cale pushing their way toward him. They arrived just in time to help hoist the winner's blanket of flowers up onto Sonya's withers. The weight of the blanket felt good on Manolin's legs, and he grinned as Cale gave the filly a big hug while cameras flashed from all sides.

Soon, Lilly and Pop joined the celebration as well. Ben saw his father and quickly grabbed him in a tight hug.

"Thank you," he told him. "For everything."

Pop smiled and pulled out his ticket. "Thank *you*," he said. "Two-hundred fifty-seven bucks at eighty-to-one . . . that's over twenty thousand dollars."

Cale grinned, happy to see her father and grandfather smiling at each other. As she returned her attention to the filly, who was prancing proudly in the midst of the chaos, she saw Balon pushing through the crowd holding . . . a hot dog?

She understood a moment later when he handed

the hot dog up to Manolin. Manny accepted it with a grateful smile, immediately taking a big bite.

Laughing, Cale turned and scanned the crowd. Her eyes finally found Prince Sadir Abal, who was sitting in one of the box seats. Seeing her look, he broke into a huge smile, then stood and offered Cale a wave and a slight bow of respect.

Cale returned both the smile and the bow. Then she waved at him happily.

Turning back, she saw that Balon had been cornered by reporters. "Two questions," one of them said, speaking rapidly. "Will Sonador run in the Dubai World Cup? And how will your team spend the three million dollars you just won?"

Balon stared at the reporter blankly. "We just won three million dollars?"

Suddenly the truth seemed to dawn on him. He grabbed the startled reporter, giving him a big hug.

Nearby, a swarm of reporters surrounded someone else at the edge of the crowd. After a second, Cale saw Everett Palmer step forward from their midst. Cale's father seemed surprised when Palmer grabbed him for a brisk handshake as cameras snapped all around them.

"So, Ben," Palmer said with his smoothest fake smile. "What's it gonna cost me now? I'd like to buy back in. What does a million get me?"

Leaving Sonya for a moment, Cale leaped toward

him. "Mr. Palmer," she said, loudly and clearly for everyone around to hear. "The first rule of horse racing is that it's not who's got the most money. It's who's got the fastest horse."

As Palmer glowered at her, speechless, Ben laughed and scooped Cale up in his arms. They were a real team — neither could have done this alone. Pop grabbed Lilly's hat and flopped it onto his own head, grinning madly. Balon danced nearby, crooning a Spanish love song. In the midst of all the people who believed in her stood Sonya, the first filly to win the Classic in the history of the Breeders' Cup.

Manolin jumped down, and Cale took his place in the saddle as flashbulbs popped. Ben proudly led them in a triumphant walk. Cale grinned so hard she thought her face might split in two. She carefully reached forward to give a proud pat to her best friend.

Everything changed that day. Not just for Sonya, or for Cale. But for the Crane Horse Farm. Before long, a fresh coat of paint had spruced up the house. The yard and paddocks were trimmed of weeds.

But those weren't the most important changes. What made the biggest difference in making the old place new again were the horses, sleek and happy, grazing in the yard or nibbling hay in their stalls . . . and the sense of hope and happiness drifting in the warm Kentucky breeze.

Get a free small popcorn with the purchase of two tickets to

Dreamer

Inspired by a true story

at participating Loews, Magic Johnson and Star Theatres.

For specific theatres and showtimes, please log onto
www.enjoytheshow.com

Present this book page and ticket stubs at the concession stand of participating
Loews Cineplex Entertainment theatres to receive your free popcorn.